FLIGHT
TO
YESTERDAY

FLIGHT
TO
YESTERDAY

Velda Johnston

G.K.HALL&CO.
Boston, Massachusetts
1990

Published in Large Print by arrangement with
St. Martin's Press.

British Commonwealth rights courtesy of Blassingame-Spectrum Corporation.

G.K. Hall Large Print Book Series.

Set in 18 pt. Plantin.

Library of Congress Cataloging-in-Publication Data

Johnston, Velda.
    Flight to yesterday / Velda Johnston.
       p.   cm. — (G.K. Hall large print book series)
     ISBN 0-8161-5055-9
     1. Large type books. I. Title. II. Series.
[PS3560.O394F55 1990b]
813'.54—dc20
                                                  90-39449

For my brother-in-law, Bud Paulson, to whom I owe the idea for this novel.

1

One swift but searching look around the big room showed me that at this hour, ten-forty in the morning, Sammy's Hamburger Haven was almost empty. A man with a Teamsters' Union button on his billed blue cap sat at the counter, elbows spread as he wolfed down scrambled eggs. About a dozen people sat at the square tables or in booths upholstered in brown vinyl. At least half of them were elderly. That did not surprise me—inside the glass front door, a sign just above the HELP WANTED notice had read, ENJOY OUR SENIOR CITIZENS' SPECIALS.

The soft strains of an old Beach Boys number filled the room. Aware of the pulse thudding in the hollow of my throat, I wondered if the music was on tape or radio. If the latter, then my name almost surely would be mentioned in the next news bulletin. But, thank God, there was no TV set—at least not visible to me.

A few feet inside the entrance a sign on a

wooden stand read, PLEASE WAIT TO BE SEATED. I walked past it to the cash register desk. Behind it stood a blond woman in her late forties, frowning down at an open ledger. She raised her head and looked at me from harried gray eyes behind pink-rimmed glasses.

"If you'll wait a moment, someone will seat you."

I set down my tote bag of heavy blue denim. "I'm not a customer. I came to apply for a job."

I did not wonder at the sudden leap of pleasure in her tired face. According to the press, fast-food restaurants all over the country were eager to hire almost anyone, from teenagers to old-age pensioners, who would be willing to serve hamburgers and draw coffee in return for the minimum wage.

"Have you had any restaurant experience?" the woman said. Her tone seemed to add that the answer wouldn't matter much.

"No."

"Have you ever worked anywhere?"

"No." A lie, but a necessary one.

"How old are you?"

"Twenty." Another lie. But thanks to a short, slightly tilted nose, I hoped I could get away with shaving four years off my age.

"What's your name?"

"Sara Blanding." I had felt it would be safe to change only my last name, rather than try to accustom myself to a new given name as well. And Sara is common enough.

"How is it, Sara, that you have never worked?"

As I had driven here from the Tattinger Institute for Women—fast, but not too fast, lest I draw the attention of a cruising police car—I had anticipated that question. Should I say I was a college student? No, why should a college student, in February, be applying for any kind of a full-time job, let alone the sort of job usually filled by those who had at most a high school diploma?

I said, "I—I've been needed at home."

Perhaps, sensing some unhappy domestic circumstance, she was restrained by delicacy from pursuing the subject. More likely, she was just too much in need of employees, almost any sort of employees. Anyway, her next question was, "Do you live here in Los Cerritos?"

"No, I'm from San Jimenez. I'm staying here with friends."

Again she did not pursue the topic. "All right, Sara." She reached under the counter and came up with a printed form. "We'll sit

3

down in a booth, and I'll get you started on your application." Dismay must have shown in my face, because she added, "You won't have to wait for the main office to okay your application. That could take weeks. I mean, the main office is short-handed too."

Good, I thought. With any luck, by the time my application was processed, I wouldn't need this job.

She went on, "In the meantime, you'll be paid off the books. The main office furnishes us a contingency fund for that. Not strictly legal, of course, but these days, if you're to stay in business at all—" She paused briefly. "You can go to work tomorrow morning. We're open twenty-four hours a day, but it's on this shift that we need help the most, six in the morning until after lunch."

She needed it, all right, even with these few customers. Only one waitress hurried about among the booths and tables. She wore a plain brown skirt and printed blouse— evidently the establishment's uniform, because the blond woman wore the same thing. From the booth where we sat I could see two male cooks behind their high counter. Plates of cooling food sat on the counter, waiting for the waitress to pick them up.

4

"Would the six A.M. shift be all right with you?"

I nodded. Anything would be all right with me, as long as it enabled me to get by for the next three weeks. Surely by then the police would have stopped watching that house, and it would be safe for me to go there.

The woman said, handing me a ballpoint pen, "My name is Marjorie Cullen. You can call me Marge. Just fill in your name, age, local address, social security number—oh, I forgot. I guess you wouldn't have a social security number, not having worked before. Well, you can apply for one."

That'll be the day, I thought.

I bent over the form. Gripping the pen hard, I wondered what to put down for a local address. Perhaps it didn't matter too much. Los Cerritos, once a sleepy agricultural village forty miles north of Los Angeles, had swollen to a city of more than a hundred thousand, a city filled with shopping malls, fast-food restaurants, and ever-expanding housing developments. Obviously this woman could not know the names of all the streets here. Just make up a name and number, I told myself. Ninety-five Blanco Way would do.

Hoping my hand would not shake visibly, I began to fill in the blanks. Why hadn't Marge Cullen returned to her ledger? I looked up.

The gray eyes were staring at me.

Surely, surely, she had not recognized me. My hair, still a little damp from the liquid tint I had applied in a service station restroom, was definitely brown now, not dark blond. Thanks to contact lenses, my eyes were brown rather than blue. And over the past four years prison food had added several pounds to my once very thin body.

Yes, I felt almost sure that I was considerably changed in appearance. But enough so? After all, those newspaper photographs hadn't recorded my coloring, only the cast of my features, and *that* hadn't changed. As for the TV cameras, I usually had managed to hide my face from them, although a few times they had caught me unaware.

The newspaper and TV coverage of my trial had been intense. "The young Jean Harris," some journalists had called me, because, like Mrs. Harris, I was charged with having killed my lover, a fashionable doctor. But Manuelo Covarrubias was not a diet expert like Jean Harris's Dr. Tarnower. He was a plastic surgeon.

6

There was another difference between Jean Harris and me. I had never confessed to killing my lover.

And I had not confessed because I was not guilty. No matter how damning the circumstances—circumstances that I could not explain, even to myself—I was not the one who had killed him.

As I sat there, forcing myself to meet Marge Cullen's puzzled gaze, she gave a little laugh. "*Now* I know who you remind me of. A second cousin of mine. A little older and a little heavier than you, but the same big brown eyes and the same shape face. Heart-shaped, I guess you'd call it. Well, I'd better get back to the counter."

When she had left me I turned, badly shaken, to gaze for a few seconds out the plate-glass window beside me. Along the boulevard, only twenty feet away beyond a narrow sidewalk and a strip of parking, cars passed in an almost bumper-to-bumper stream. I turned and looked across the room, through more plate glass, at a Ford dealer's lot out there, packed with shiny vehicles of a half-dozen different hues. I saw a long, low, white-stucco building, probably a garage, and beyond that a line of royal palms, their green feather-duster tops swaying in the breeze. In the distance, a range of coastal mountains rose dark blue against the bright winter sky.

This was the California people all over the world visualized, a land of ever-blooming roses, of freeways so broad and crowded that from a quarter of a mile away their roar sounded like Niagara's.

This was not my California. Mine was many miles to the north. I thought of redwood forests, utterly silent because their insect-proof wood offered no attraction to birds. I thought of mountain towns that had changed little in the past hundred years, and of snow-filled canyons blue with afternoon shadows. And, of course, I thought of my mother.

An almost physical pain wrenched my heart. Quickly I bent over the printed form.

As I wrote, I was vaguely aware that two more waitresses had arrived, undoubtedly for the lunch-through-early-dinner shift. The booths and tables were filling up, and more customers stood behind the wait-to-be-seated sign.

No news bulletins or commercials had interrupted the music. It was on tape, then. A small circumstance, but it gave me hope that luck was with me.

When I finished the form I sat there in the booth, waiting for a moment when Marge would not be dealing with either arriving or departing customers. Finally, I walked over to her and laid the form beside the cash register.

She looked up from her ledger. "Finished? Good. Now better be here a little before six tomorrow morning. I'll have a uniform ready for you. You're a size ten, right?"

I nodded.

She placed my application form in some recess below the counter. "Then I'll see you tomorrow, Sara."

I said, "There's one other thing—"

"Just a moment, Sara."

I waited for her to accept a lunch check from two elderly women and ring up the sale. Then I said, "My friends can't put me up any longer, and I need a place to stay. Do you know of anything around here, something inexpensive?"

Head tilted to one side, she considered. "That's a tough one. Any sort of place is scarce right now. Lots of Easterners out here for the winter, you know. Offhand, I can't—" Her face brightened. "The motel! It's right next door."

9

A motel. Probably at least forty dollars a night. I felt dismay.

Tattinger Institute for Women is a model prison. In fact, some punitive-minded individuals refer to it as a "country club prison," allowing far too many comforts and privileges to the female felons within its tan stucco walls. Prisoners can not only make money but spend it—on candy, record players, magazine subscriptions, TV sets, or anything else on the list of approved purchases.

I had worked in the prison's kitchen, first as a scrubber of copper-bottomed pots and a scraper of plates for the dishwasher, later as a vegetable peeler and salad maker. Still later, I had been assigned to the library. I had spent some of my modest earnings—no minimum wage laws for convicted felons— but I'd saved some, too. And, to the tight-lipped disapproval of the matron in charge of our savings, I had withdrawn half of that—about three hundred dollars—as soon as I had made up my mind that I must get out of the place.

"Marge, I can't afford a motel."

"You can afford this one. The owner's redoing all the rooms at one end of the second floor. Some of them are already finished, and I hear he's renting those for ten a night.

Of course, there are painters and carpenters swarming all over that part of the motel in the daytime, but you wouldn't be there much then.

"Oh—and did I tell you that you can have your meals here at half price?"

I shook my head.

"Well, you can. Even dinner, although that's not on your shift."

I heard a whooshing sound behind me and knew that the revolving door had been pushed into motion. Marge's face had already assumed its welcoming-hostess smile. "Good afternoon, folks. Will it be smoking or non-smoking?" Then, to me: "See you in the morning, Sara."

Out on the sidewalk, tote bag in hand, I paused for a moment. The famous California sunlight poured down on the endless stream of cars and on the Ford lot next door, where dressed-for-success young salesmen lounged, arms crossed, against the shiny new vehicles, waiting for customers. They were uniformly tall and good-looking, and I had a hunch that they were also waiting for someone from the movie and TV industry to discover them.

It seemed to me that the sunlight had taken on a brassy tinge, and that there was a slightly metallic smell in the air. Automobile fumes mingling with fog particles from the nearby ocean? Or Los Angeles smog creeping north into Ventura County?

A police car passed. Neither of the uniformed men in it looked at me, but my heart gave a panicky leap nevertheless.

I looked to my right. A large sign revolved atop a tall pole: RESTWELL MOTEL. I turned and walked rapidly toward it.

2

The motel's office had a front wall of plate glass. Through it I could see a man standing behind the counter, propped on his elbows, fists balled against his cheeks as he read an outspread newspaper. I drew a deep breath and pushed the door open.

He raised his head. He was about twenty-six, I judged, with bristly dark brown hair cut almost as short as a marine's. He had a craggy face with a prow-like nose and cold gray eyes. According to the nameplate on the desk, he, or at least someone, was Michael Rolfe, Manager.

He gave me no greeting whatsoever. My

genial host, I thought. "Good afternoon," I said.

He nodded.

It has never even occurred to me to enter a beauty contest, still the look in masculine eyes, as well as what I see in my own mirror, have told me that I am reasonably attractive. So why the cold expression from this man? Stomach knotting, I wondered if he had recognized me instantly. Of course not, I told myself. It wasn't that sort of expression. But had he sensed that there was something "not right" about me? Perhaps. Yet, his aloofness seemed too impersonal for that.

"The manager of the restaurant next door said that you had some inexpensive rooms."

Again he nodded and then, looking past me at the motel's empty driveway, asked, "Where's your car?"

Now being carless definitely *was* something "not right," especially in California, where babies are born with hands curved to hold a steering wheel.

"It broke down. It's in a garage now."

"How long will you be staying?"

"I—I don't know. Until I can find an apartment, I suppose." I paused. "Tomorrow I start work at Sammy's Hamburger Haven."

13

That did seem to startle him, although he didn't say why. I went on. "Could you tell me how much your rooms are, Mr. Rolfe? Marge Cullen said something about ten dollars a night."

He didn't correct me, so apparently he *was* Michael Rolfe. "That's right, Miss—"

"Blanding. Sara Blanding."

It was not a name I had snatched out of mid-air. Josiah Blanding, an ancestor of my father's on the maternal side, had been the nearest thing to a famous person of which my family could boast. Late in the last century he had achieved considerable success as a concert pianist. It was the conviction that I had inherited his talent, which had impelled my mother to drive herself endlessly, holding down two jobs to pay for my music lessons, even though I had known from the age of twelve onward that I would never have anything more than a knack to play pleasant music for my friends, or, at most, for the patrons of some cocktail lounge.

"All right, Miss Blanding. I'll show you the room."

I followed him outside, and along a cement walk that led past a stand of multi-colored rose bushes to the motel itself. This was L-shaped, with iron stairs leading up to

14

the walkway in front of its second-story rooms. On the short leg of the L, out on the walkway, a man in white painter's overalls bent over a tall pail, evidently mixing its contents. I could hear men's voices, and the sound of hammering, and some deafening heavy-metal rock music.

I followed my guide along the walkway past the long row of closed doors. To my right, beyond the parking lot whose yellow lines marked each guest's assigned space, I could see a swimming pool enclosed by a high wire-mesh fence.

We passed the man with the pail—it contained light green paint, I saw—and the open door of a room where two other workmen, on their knees, hammered at something. The next door was closed. Michael Rolfe turned a key in its lock and swung the door back. I stepped past him into the room.

Light green walls, darker green carpet. A pleasant floral bedspread, and matching draw draperies at the floor-to-ceiling front windows.

"Dressing room and bath through there," he said.

I inspected them. Everything seemed spotlessly clean and fresh. When I returned to him I said, "It all looks brand new."

15

"It practically is. New carpet, new paint on the walls, new bathroom tile. The crew finished with this room just yesterday. Are you allergic to fresh paint?"

"I don't know."

"If you are, you'll find out soon enough. You'll up-chuck, or maybe break out in hives."

When it came to renting his accommodations, I thought, he could scarcely be called a master salesman. In spite of my own anxieties, I felt curious about his attitude.

"You don't like your job much, do you?"

"What job?"

"Why, running this motel."

"That's not a job. I mean, I'm the owner until I can get it off my hands." When I didn't say anything, he went on, "And if you're wondering why I bought it in the first place, the answer is I didn't. An uncle left it to me. I quit my job with a Los Angeles stockbroker so I could whip this place into shape and sell it."

"And then what? Back to the stock-brokerage?"

"Hell, no. I was working there just to try to make enough money to do what I really want to do—get into law school before I'm too damned old."

16

He paused and then went on gloomily, "Up until my sophomore year at UCLA, I thought I was going to try to be a writer. Maybe I should have stuck with that idea. You don't need four years of graduate school to be a writer."

"Why not try to combine the two?"

"You mean like Louis Auchincloss? I think I'll probably try. Although it's non-fiction that appeals to me, not novels. Maybe someday I'll write a book called *My Ten Most Memorable Cases*, or some such. Well, you want the room? Ten bucks a night."

I winced. Someone had turned up the already deafening volume of that tape player or radio. Well, these workmen wouldn't arrive in the mornings until after I'd gone to my job. And after I was off work, I could lie on one of the yellow chaise longues by the pool over there, or maybe just walk around the neighborhood. . . .

No! Best to stay out of sight, thus minimizing the chances of being recognized. I had to work—how else could I survive?—but when off duty I'd stay in my room as much as possible, racket or no racket.

"I'll take it," I said.

He laid the key on the long table of blond wood, built-in against one wall. "I'll leave

17

this here. When you get ready, come down and register."

I thought he would leave then. Instead he asked, "Are you going to eat at Sammy's?"

"Of course. As an employee, I can eat for half-price."

"Take my advice. Even if you have to cut down to a meal a day, eat somewhere else. The food at Sammy's may not kill you, but my hunch is it takes years off your life."

He started toward the door and then stopped, looking down at my tote bag. "Is that your only luggage?"

It was. All my other clothing remained behind the walls of the Tattinger Institute. I had not dared to take more than the tote bag. Jammed down inside it were two pairs of pantyhose, a nightgown and cotton robe, and a denim skirt and blue cotton T-shirt. In my handbag I'd placed a toothbrush and a small can of tooth powder.

"No," I said. "I left a suitcase at a friend's house."

He looked at me. Was there a stir of suspicion in that bony, unsmiling face? I couldn't be sure. "Okay," he said. "See you."

He went out, closing the door behind him. Seconds later, the blare of rock music softened to a murmur. Evidently, on my behalf, he had asked to have the volume lowered. I couldn't be sure, of course, but maybe that meant he didn't distrust me, despite my carless and luggageless state. And maybe he was not the dour character I had taken him for at first. Maybe he was just a would-be lawyer stuck temporarily in a business he hated.

I looked at my watch. Less than a minute before one. Quickly, I went to the TV set, turned the switch, punched a button. I knew a Los Angeles channel carried a one o'clock news program.

The sound came on first. "—Marsden, warden of the women's prison, announced late this morning." I could see the announcer now, a red-haired man of about forty. "Sara Hargreaves, until then a model prisoner, had been assigned to drive an injured member of the prison staff to her weekly physical therapy session in Los Viejos, a nearby town. Miss Hargreaves left the patient at the doctor's office and then, instead of waiting for her, drove off in the car, a light gray Chevrolet sedan, which is prison property.

"Miss Hargreaves was convicted almost four years ago of killing her lover, Dr. Manuelo Covarrubias, a fashionable plastic surgeon who owned the Serena Sanatorium in the San Joaquin Valley. She has been serving a four-to-twelve-year sentence at Tattinger, an experimental prison that follows many of the lenient practices first tried out in Scandinavia. The judge who presided at her trial cited her youth—she was twenty years old at the time—and the circumstantial nature of the evidence against her as reasons for the comparative lightness of her sentence."

An inset still-picture had appeared in one corner of the screen. It was a photograph of me taken during my trial. "Sara Hargreaves is now twenty-four years old, with ash-blond hair and blue eyes. Her height is five-feet-five. Her weight is a hundred eighteen pounds, five pounds more than when she entered prison."

The announcer gave the license number of that gray Chevrolet sedan—the car I had left on a quiet street several blocks from this motel—and then said, "Anyone seeing Miss Hargreaves or the car is urged to notify the police immediately.

"In the latest damage suit against a major tobacco company, lawyers for the plaintiff argued today in a Los Angeles courtroom—"

I turned off the set. Hands spread flat on the built-in table, I stared into the mirror that hung above it. I was seeing not just my reflected image, in the green sweater and white duck pants I had put on in my room at Tattinger that morning. I was also seeing that inset photo of my face on the TV screen—a thin face, almost gaunt, with blue eyes that looked very large and blondish hair that nearly reached my shoulders. It had been a face that looked younger than twenty, not just because of the slightly turned-up nose, but because of the mouth, soft and vulnerable, that had seemed to tremble with fear even in that still photograph.

Surely I no longer closely resembled my twenty-year-old self, and not just because of the five extra pounds and the brown contact lenses. My mouth was different now, firmer, more disciplined. And my once ash-blond hair was not only dark now, but shaped close to my head.

I had been given the new hairdo by one of the other "girls" at Tattinger, a forty-five-year-old beautician who, tired of the black eyes and split lips frequently given her by her husband, had pushed him out a third-story window, breaking both his legs. Goaded on the witness stand into saying that she had hoped to break not his legs but his neck, she had received a three-year sentence.

21

I had been easily persuaded to let her cut my hair. In fact, it was only because of Manuelo's objections that I had not cut it earlier.

Yes, I told myself, I had a good chance of remaining at large for three weeks. By then the police, waiting for me in vain at that house deep in the winter wood, would conclude that I had fled the state, or perhaps even the country. Then I could go to the one person on earth that I loved, and stay with her until the end.

My mother had had so little out of life. Hard work, and widowhood, and disappointment that I had not turned out to have the talent that she, in her adoring pride, had attributed to me. Most terrible of all, of course, had been my arrest and conviction. Frightened as I had been at my trial, and embittered as I had felt at times during my years at Tattinger, I never for a moment doubted that my mother had suffered more than I. I would not let her spend the last weeks of her life alone.

Quite suddenly, the tension of the last few hours gave way to leaden fatigue. I moved to the window and drew the draperies closed. Then I walked to the bed and fell onto it, fully clothed. Despite the sounds of hammering, and the subdued but still audible music, I fell asleep almost immediately.

Hours later I awoke to see the last glimmer of daylight coming through the crack between the drapes. Still groggy, I undressed and put on the cotton nightgown from my tote bag. I turned on the light above the bedside table that held a clock radio, and I set the alarm for five. A hollow feeling in my midriff reminded me that I'd had no food since breakfast. But I was still more tired than hungry.

I got into bed, turned off the light, and went back to sleep.

3

When I next awoke I found myself in inky darkness. For a moment I didn't even know where I was. Then I remembered. I looked at the luminous dial of my watch: Four-ten. No wonder that after all those hours of sleep, I had awakened before the alarm went off.

I got out of bed, crossed over the carpet to the window, and drew the draperies slightly apart. The yellow glow of tall standing lamps fell on the parking lot. Almost empty when I fell asleep the previous afternoon, it was now nearly full. I saw several trucks, including an enormous diesel rig. Its shiny blue cab and aluminum trailer stretched across several parking spaces beside the fenced-in swimming pool. I must have been deeply asleep indeed not to have heard its arrival.

In the bathroom I took a long hot shower and then dressed in the denim skirt and blue T-shirt from my tote bag. Glad that I had awakened early, I washed my white duck pants and hung them over the shower rod to dry. Somehow I must contrive to get one more change of clothing.

By the time I stepped from my room onto the walkway, that range of mountains was taking shape in the dawn light. Below me, in the parking lot, a man in a natty three-piece suit was putting what looked like a salesman's sample case onto the rear seat of his sedan.

I locked my door and dropped the key into my shoulder bag. I descended the iron stairs and moved along the walk that ran past the motel's lighted office. A youth with carroty hair, evidently the motel's night man, sat on what must have been a high stool behind the counter, his face propped up on one hand, his eyes closed. Suddenly I remembered that

I had not registered. Should I do so now? No, apparently there was no rush. Otherwise Michael Rolfe would have returned to my room yesterday afternoon or telephoned me. It could wait until I finished my shift.

In the growing light, I went out to the sidewalk and turned left. Evidently the morning rush hour already had started. Cars, many with their headlights still on, moved along the highway in a steady stream. I had a brief, jumbled memory of my growing up years. That house, deep in the pines. That little town with its silver mine, which didn't produce much ore now, only enough to keep the town alive. Maybe it was the quiet of my early surroundings that made me find traffic-clogged highways not only unpleasant but actually depressing.

When I entered Sammy's, Marge Cullen was already standing behind the register. The restaurant, I saw, was much busier than it had been when I first entered it late the previous morning. At least at the counter. About a dozen truckers, some of whom probably had spent the night in the motel, sat on the row of stools.

"You're early," Marge greeted me. "Want your breakfast?"

Did I! Ever since I woke up I had been

25

aware of my empty stomach's growls of complaint. "Yes, please."

"Well, I'll show you where you can change into your uniform. Then you can come out to a table and order anything you want. Afterwards I'll explain your job to you."

As I followed her along an aisle between the tables, she asked over her shoulder, "Get fixed up at the motel all right?"

"Yes."

"Good." She opened a door in the big room's rear wall. "Here's where you change."

I entered a small room containing six narrow lockers. Beyond, through an open doorway, were a wash basin and stall with a lattice door. Marge nodded at a brown skirt and floral-print blouse on a hanger at one end of the row of lockers. "There's your uniform." She opened one of the lockers and handed me the key. "Put your handbag and street clothes in your locker, and keep the key in your uniform pocket. We've had some thefts here. Well, I'd better get back to the desk."

A few minutes later, in uniform, I sat at a small table at the rear of the restaurant. A similarly uniformed waitress, a Mexican girl who was too fat but had a pretty, dimpled

26

face, gave me a comradely smile as she handed me a menu.

Mindful of what Michael Rolfe had said about the food, I decided to resist the "Down Home Breakfast with scrambled eggs, sizzling country sausage, and crisp hash brown potatoes," even though the words alone without the accompanying illustration would have made my mouth water. "I'll have grapefruit juice, corn flakes, buttered toast, and coffee," I said. Surely nothing could go wrong with that order.

The "freshly squeezed" grapefruit juice, when the waitress brought it, obviously had been poured from a can, but that didn't matter. The corn flakes, which arrived in a small, one-serving box, tasted the way corn flakes always do. And the coffee was actually good—hot and strong and fresh. But the butter-smeared toast was a different story. Except for carbon-black grill marks, the bread was almost as pale as it must have been when it came out of the wrapper. It took some sort of perverted genius, I decided, to turn out toast like that.

When I had finished breakfast, Marge, in her phrase, "showed me the ropes." I was to draw orders of coffee and tea from the urns in front of the chefs" counter. From the same area, I was to dip ice cream from the rows of freezers. And, I was to take servings of Danish from a case next to the freezers. If the customer wanted the confection hot, then I was to hand it to one of the chefs to heat in the microwave.

When I placed an order before a customer, I was to smile and say, "*There* we go!" Marge said that customers, especially the seniors, seemed to like that. Perhaps, I reflected, the phrase made them feel that a meal at Sammy's was an adventure, something like a short cruise.

The place was quite busy, and it grew more so during the lunch hours. It was a good thing. Trying to keep my orders straight, and rushing between the chefs' counter and the tables to attempt to serve the food hot (or at least warm), I didn't have much time to worry about whether some customers stared at me merely because I was new, or because they found something familiar in my appearance.

Once, when I picked up orders from the counter and looked inside the kitchen at the two sullen-looking men flipping hamburgers on a greasy grill, I thought of the kitchen at Tattinger: All stainless steel and shiny linoleum and butcher clock counters, it would have been a pleasant place to work had it not been part of a prison, a place you could not walk away from. Except that I *had* walked away, or rather, driven.

I thought of the gray sedan I had left parked in front of a vacant lot several blocks from here. Had it been reported to the police yet? I hoped not. I had left it on a street of fairly new but inexpensive houses, the sort of neighborhood where most wives as well as their husbands were probably away at work. Days might pass with each householder thinking that one of his neighbors had parked the Chevy there. But it did no good to think about it. Carrying a plate of hamburger-with-fries in each hand, I hurried toward a booth.

At two o'clock I changed into my denim skirt and blue T-shirt, put my uniform in my locker, and went out into the restaurant's main room for my half-priced lunch. A tall, raw-boned girl, working the early-afternoon-through-dinner shift, handed me a menu.

I looked dubiously down the list of colorfully described, and sometimes attractively illustrated, menu items. My eye lit upon "stuffed broiled pork chops, accompanied by delicious vegetables of the season."

Surely that would be safe. They had a microwave here. The chops might turn out to be overdone, but certainly not underdone. No restaurant would dare to serve half-raw pork.

But when the food came, one glance showed me I had miscalculated. Like the morning's toast, the chops bore charred grill marks. Otherwise they were of uniform gray. The first taste confirmed my impression that they had been baked days before, stuffed with a bread mixture, and put in the freezer. When I gave my order, one of the cooks had simply heated them in the microwave.

"The delicious vegetable of the season" was a small bowl of lukewarm canned green beans.

A few minutes later, when I walked up front to pay my check, the red-haired woman who had taken Marge Cullen's place for the afternoon shift asked, "Enjoy your lunch, dear?"

"Yes." Those pork chops weren't her fault.

She rang up $2.68. "Coming back tonight for dinner?"

"I'm not sure what I'll do."

But as I stepped out into the sunlight, I realized grimly that I had better try to put up with those half-priced meals. Money was going to be important to me. For one thing, I'd need a car.

When I reached the motel office, I saw that its reluctant owner was on duty. He sat in a swivel chair behind the counter, feet up on a desk, a heavy volume open in his hands. When I came into the office he got up and walked over to the counter, still holding the book.

"I didn't register yesterday."

"I know." He had laid the book down on the counter. I saw that it was *Constitutional Law*, by someone named Joseph Edwards.

"I meant to come down here yesterday afternoon, but I fell asleep."

"I know," he said again. When I looked at him with surprise, he added, "When I checked that room last Tuesday I noticed there was no bath mat. Since the maids had already gone home by the time you checked in, I brought the mat up myself. You didn't answer my knock, so I concluded you'd gone out someplace. It never occurred to me that you could go to sleep with all that racket going on. But there you were, out like a light. I put the mat in the bathroom and left."

For a moment I just looked at him. Was

it really because of the bathmat that he had used his key to my room? Or had he decided to do a little snooping?

Stop it, I told myself. True, I needed to be alert for any sign of danger, but I must not become paranoid.

I said aloud, "I was very tired last night." It had been more than the nerve strain of that morning. For several nights before I left Tattinger I had slept scarcely at all. Instead I had listened to my roommate's light snores, watched on the ceiling the refracted glow of a prison yard floodlight, and thought of all the things that could go wrong—

Rolfe's gray eyes seemed to be studying me. Was he wondering why I had been tired enough to sleep in "all that racket"? I asked quickly, "Where is your register?"

"Just fill out this card."

I wrote, "Sara Blanding, San Jimenez, California." The San Jimenez part wasn't a complete misstatement. I had attended the musical academy there.

That morning it had occurred to me to try to disguise my handwriting when I registered. But no. If the police managed to trace me to this motel, a registration card with a false name written in a disguised hand wouldn't help me. All they would have to

32

do was to ask if a young woman, probably carless, had registered at the motel recently.

Besides, if I filled out the card slowly and carefully, it might strike this bony-faced man as still another odd thing about me.

He took the card and placed it in a gray metal file on the counter. "Do you want to pay by the day or week?"

"The week, I guess."

"Okay."

I was about to turn away when he asked, "Did you eat at Sammy's?"

"Breakfast and lunch."

"How was it?"

"Just as you said. Except for the coffee, the cooking ran from bad to unspeakable."

"Then how about having dinner down here tonight?"

"Down here?"

"My apartment is in back of this office. I'm a good cook. And, I've got abalone steaks in the fridge."

Why? I thought. Why should he ask me to dinner, someone for whom he had manifested no visible liking only the day before? Had he decided that he did like me, after all? Or did he want to try to verify a suspicion that there was something wrong about me?

"Take that look off your face," he said.

"I'm not planning to pounce—not right away, at least. For one thing, I'll still be on duty. Lots of people check in during the early evening. I'll have to leave the door open between my apartment and the office."

He added, "I also have a pretty good Chablis. Well?"

If he did suspect that there was something wrong about me, shying away from his invitation might only strengthen that suspicion. Besides, when I weighed the prospect of Sammy's menu against abalone steak . . .

"Thank you, Mr. Rolfe. That sounds very nice."

"People I ask to dinner call me Mike. Why don't you come down here around seven o'clock?"

4

The white duck pants I had hung in my bathroom before daylight that morning were dry. These, plus my yellow sweater, would hardly make a festive outfit, but it would have to do. Tomorrow afternoon, I told myself gloomily, I would have to spend a few of my precious dollars on clothes and a suitcase, preferably a secondhand one.

At five the workmen loaded their ladders, paint buckets, hammers, and radio into a truck and left. I lay on the bed, listening to a local radio station that broadcast news summaries every half hour. The bulletins concerning me merely rehashed those of the day before—which might, or might not, mean that the police had garnered no more information. At seven I went downstairs.

Mike's apartment consisted of one large room plus an alcove kitchen. I suspected that it was his uncle who had selected the wall-to-wall gray carpet and the chunky sofa bed and armchair, both covered in a dull green material with a metallic stripe. But I was sure that Mike himself had added the shelves of books along one wall, and also, probably, the nice old gateleg table, now set for two with straw mats, white china, and wine glasses.

The walls were decorated with matted photographs of mountain scenes—snow-laden pines; a foamy waterfall plunging into a forest pool; a fox leaving tracks as it crossed a snow-covered meadow. With the quick apprehension of the fugitive, I was sure for a few moments that these pictures had been taken somewhere in the vicinity of Oresburg, The little mountain town where I had grown up. But when I ventured to ask, Mike told me that he had taken the photographs while on a skiing holiday at a friend's condo in Aspen, Colorado.

Several times, while he presided at the stove in the alcove, the ring of the desk bell summoned him to the office. Three times during our meal, too, he left the table to check in a guest. The interruptions did not keep me from enjoying the expertly sauced abalone steak, the tender asparagus, or the new potatoes cooked in their jackets.

After dinner, though, when we sat on the sofa, with small glasses of brandy on the coffee table before us, the bell did not ring. "Probably nobody else will arrive tonight," Mike said. "This place mostly gets truckers and traveling businessmen, guys who check in early and check out early.

"Maybe that's what makes the business so dull," he went on gloomily. "It's all just leaky faucets and maids who don't show up for work and guys with union buttons or sample cases. Sometimes I wish Uncle Ed had left me one of those hot-pillow joints with X-rated movies available in every room." He laughed, evidently struck by some incongruity in the idea of his late uncle running such a place. Then gloom again settled over his face. "At least the customers would be more interesting."

"Well, you'll probably be able to sell the place soon."

"I hope so. I've been accepted at Stanford Law School next fall. One of the top experts on Constitutional law teaches there, you know."

"No, I didn't know."

"That's the aspect of law that has always interested me. Not just the various interpretations of what our Constitution says, but tracing the ideas in it—the inviolability of a man's dwelling place, for instance—back through history to the old Greeks. Somehow criminal law never appealed to me."

Criminal law. Criminal courts. The gauntlet of TV cameramen and shouting reporters I'd had to run each time I entered or left that courthouse. My sense of kinship with all caught, helpless things—the broken-winged bird carried in a cat's mouth, the beaver struggling in a trap—as I sat there in that courtroom. Worst of all, the look on my mother's deathly-white face as, after the sentencing, a policewoman grasped my arm and led me away.

"Did you grow up here in Los Cerritos?" I had asked it unthinkingly, trying to blot out those pictures in my mind. As soon as the words left my tongue, I regretted them. Asking him about his background was to invite questions about my own.

"No, I grew up in Anaheim."

He went on to say that his had been a large family, four brothers and a sister. "My father has always made good money—he's an architect—but with that many children he couldn't afford to spend too much educating any single one of us. There was enough to pay my way through UCLA, with me working at summer jobs. But I had my heart set on going to Stanford for my law degree. That's why I worked in a broker's office until Uncle Ed left me this place."

He went on talking easily of what it had been like growing up with four other boys and a girl. The basketball team, Rolfes' Ramblers, which they had organized when Joey, the youngest, had reached the age of eight. The noisy, amiably argumentative family dinners. The mingled adoration and envy they had felt for Nancy, the over-indulged only girl of the family.

Four brothers and a sister. While with one part of my mind I listened to him, with another part I thought of my own often-solitary

38

childhood, much of it spent in a house deep in the pine forest above Oresburg.

Not that I had been born there. My father had bought the house when I was two years old. I had been born in Oakland, that poor relation of regal San Francisco. My mother and father had met at the Oakland Furniture Wholesalers, where they had both worked as bookkeepers.

It was while they were on a vacation trip in a rented RV that they discovered the little mining town of Oresburg and decided to spend a few days in its vicinity. I remember nothing of that trip, of course. But my mother told me of how one morning my father had left our campsite to walk into the town for a newspaper. When he returned, after an interval so long that she had begun to worry, he was full of enthusiasm. In the Bluebird Cafe, where he had stopped for coffee, he had met the assistant superintendent of Oresburg's no-longer-rich but still-producing silver mine. When the other man, John Burford, had learned my father was a bookkeeper, he had half-jokingly offered him a job. The mine's office manager, Burford said, was about to retire. At my father's display of interest, the talk turned serious.

As my father excitedly pointed out to my

mother, the pay was almost as much as he'd been receiving in Oakland, and living up here would be much cheaper. In fact, he and Burford had taken a drive into the woods to look at a house that could be bought for a few hundred dollars down. Sure, it was badly in need of repair, but he was handy with tools. And the site was beautiful—a nice big clearing with wildflowers growing in it, a bubbling spring nearby with a brook flowing from it.

And when Sara was old enough to go to school, she would be better off in Oresburg's one-room schoolhouse than in some crowded city school, with its overworked teachers and often unruly kids.

I don't think my father's main reason was any of the practical ones he gave. I think his main reason was that he had always wanted to live in a house in the woods. I don't know how many times I saw him reading *Walden Pond*. In fact, I think that with a different background and more education—like my mother, he came from poor people—he might have been some kind of scholar, or even a poet.

My mother, who adored him, soon gave in to his arguments. Thus my earliest memories are of the flash of a bluejay's wing across that woodland clearing, and the whine of the jeep my father had bought, as it carried the three of us along the snowy road leading down to the little town.

Mine was a happy childhood. I loved the summers, when I spent the long days sometimes playing in the yards of children in the town, sometimes stretched out on a blanket in the clearing, with a book in my hands. In the winter I loved school—except for arithmetic—and my teacher, Miss Brawley.

On certain Saturdays Miss Brawley asked the entire student body (which never numbered more than fourteen) to her house, where the youngest children romped noisily in the yard, the older ones played games like The Minister's Cat, and all of us, after a lunch of hot dogs, milk, and cookies, gathered around the piano and sang along to Miss Brawley's accompaniment.

On one such Saturday when I was eight, my parents were a little late in calling for me. After the other children left I went to the piano and picked out "Schooldays" with one finger. Looking strangely excited, Miss Brawley showed me how to turn that single note into a chord. When my parents arrived, she asked me to show them what I had learned.

41

As we all moved toward the door, I heard her say to my mother, "I do believe Sara has musical talent."

Fatal words. I think that instantly my mother was reminded of that concert pianist ancestor of my father's. Anyway, from that day on, she—who was anything but a nagger—began to nag. Sara must have a piano. Sara must have lessons.

She won. My father went to Oakland and bought, on time, a used upright piano. And each Saturday morning my mother drove me several miles to Leesville, another small town, to take lessons from a Mrs. Wilson. I enjoyed the lessons, and I enjoyed practicing on that old upright, which, with its marks made by wet glasses and burning cigarettes, gave evidence of service in far more lively surroundings than our small parlor. But even as a child, I had a sense that my mother's starry-eyed faith in my talent would never be justified.

The summer I was ten, my father, driving alone in the jeep between Oresburg and Leeville, had a flat tire. He pulled over to the shoulder to change it, and a car, doing seventy on the wrong side of the road, struck and killed him as he knelt there. When the state police finally caught up with the driver,

42

they found that he had been on a cocaine high and had no memory of the incident.

I think that from the day of my father's death onward, my mother did not laugh. She smiled sometimes. But that clear ringing laugh of hers—blond head thrown back, blue eyes filled with merriment—was gone forever.

There were practical matters to occupy her in her raw grief. The mine management offered her a job. It was really my father's job, although they did not call it "office manager" but "bookkeeper," and quoted a lower salary. Nevertheless, she accepted. It seemed a better solution than moving back to Oakland, where her own kinfolk were all either too poor or too elderly to help her much. Besides, the mine's manager offered her the wintertime rental of an apartment above a local store he owned, Oresburg Hardware. That was important. A woman and child could scarcely spend winters alone in that isolated woodland house.

To make up for the reduced income and the added expense of rent, my mother took on a second job. Weekends she worked as a waitress at Oresburg's only night spot, the Silver Nugget Bar and Grill. It seemed an odd sort of employment for someone as gentle as my mother. But as it turned out, that very quiet dignity of hers seemed to be her armor. I never heard that anyone made any sort of a pass at her, not the men from the mine on their weekly spree, or the local businessmen, or the tourists who stopped in, hoping that a place called the Silver Nugget would afford them a glimpse of the Old West. It was a vain hope. The nearest thing to the Old West the place offered was a pair of huge moose antlers—plastic, made in Taiwan—above the bar mirror.

"Like some music?" asked Mike Rolfe, seated beside me on his convertible sofa.

"Love it."

He went to the turntable in one corner of the room and from the wire holder before it selected a record. He put it on the turntable and came back to sit beside me. As Beethoven's mighty piano concerto the *Emperor* filled the room, I returned to thinking of my mother's stubborn delusion about my own musical ability.

She had not only insisted that I continue with my piano lessons. When I reached my senior high school year, she had begun to talk of my continuing to train at the San Jimenez Academy of Music.

"Mother, it's terribly expensive! I'd thought of going to San Jose State and majoring in English, so that later on I could teach—"

"You don't know everything about my finances, young lady! Some Saturday nights the tips at the Nugget are pretty good. Besides, there are student loans. I already wrote to the academy about it, and they said yes."

"But it's so far away!" San Jimenez, world-famous for its beautiful resort hotel, the Miraflores Inn, was a small city about a hundred miles southwest of Oresburg.

A shadow crossed her face. "I know. But the bus fare isn't much. You'll be able to come home lots of weekends." She smiled. "And anyway, I'll still have Charlie." Charlie was a part-Airedale we had acquired when I was ten and he was a six-month-old puppy.

In the end, as I should have known I would, I went to San Jimenez.

The faculty members at San Jimenez were pleasant. So were most of the students, despite a rivalry natural to any group of would-be performing artists. I soon realized that a few of them, a very few, might be famous in another ten years. A larger number might become members of symphony orchestras. The majority were like me, people with a pleasant little talent that they could use to entertain themselves and their friends.

After a few months it became apparent that even with the money my mother sent, and my small student loan, I would still need a part-time job. At the academy's student employment office, the woman looked me up in her files, leafed through another file, and then said, "Here's something! A very good job, too. The Inn needs a pianist to play during the cocktail hours each afternoon." That was what people called the Miraflores Inn, just "the Inn." "They'll want show tunes, except when a customer asks for something else, of course. You wouldn't have to worry about what to wear. They'll select clothes for you from the Inn's boutiques. And the job pays well—two hundred dollars for three hours a day, five days a week. If you play weekends, that will be another hundred."

As I listened, a certain wryness mingled with my pleasure. This job would never have been offered to one of the few really talented students. Tinkling out "Tea for Two" and such, day after day, could only harm a future concert pianist.

But when I telephoned my mother that night, she did not recognize the significance of my news. It seemed to her a confirmation of my outstanding talent.

I got the job.

The cocktail lounge at the Inn was the loveliest room I had ever seen, either in or out of the movies. Sofas and fan-back chairs, all of white wicker woven with expensive intricacy, clustered around tables covered with mosaic tiles. The dark blue carpet with a gold central medallion, woven to order in Brussels, was deep and springy underfoot. Oil paintings that depicted the hotel's famous gardens ornamented the walls. And exquisitely arranged flowers from those same gardens were everywhere, including a white wicker basket on the grand piano.

I had been playing at the Inn a little more than two weeks when I met Manuelo Covarrubias.

He left a small party of people at one end of the big room to approach the piano. "Do you know 'All the Things You Are'? Or are you too young to have even heard of it?"

People say there is no such thing as love at first sight, and I suppose they are right. An emotion as complex as love takes time to grow. But I do know one thing. A woman, as well as a man, can feel an overwhelming sexual attraction at first sight.

He was six feet or a little under, With dark, slightly curling hair, dark eyes, and a classically handsome face—straight, strong nose, sensual mouth with a full underlip, square jaw. His tan was of that deep, all-year-round color. Like many of the Inn's male guests, he wore white duck trousers, a cotton shirt open at the throat, and a blue blazer with some kind of club emblem on the pocket.

I said, "Yes, I know that one." A sensitive interpreter of Mozart I will never be, but since the age of twelve I have been able to play any melody after hearing it only once.

"Will you play it for me?"

I had a premonition—half exhilarating, half frightening—that in time I would try to do anything for him that he asked, including swim around Cape Horn. It was just as well that few guests of the Inn stayed long. At several hundred to a thousand dollars a day, few could afford to.

"Of course," I said.

"Thank you, Miss Hargreaves." So he had asked someone, probably a waiter, what my name was. He turned and walked back to his table. How old was he? In his forties, probably. That morning, if anyone had asked me, I would have said that a man of forty-odd was too old to interest a girl not yet twenty. But now the idea of his being that much older seemed to enhance something that, apart from his looks, attracted me. I suppose it was a certain sense of power that seemed to emanate from him.

I played "All the Things You Are," resisting the urge to put in fancy trills with my right hand and elaborate chords with my left. Instead I played it gently, simply.

When I'd finished, there he was again beside me. "Thank you. That was lovely." He paused. "You'll be taking a break soon, won't you?"

My pulse leaped. "At five-thirty."

"Will you join my party for a drink then?"

"Thank you. That sounds nice."

Half an hour later I walked toward his table. A red-haired woman, dressed in yellow linen, sat there with her back to me. It wasn't until my host, along with the other man at the table, had gotten to his feet and introduced me that I realized she was Elisa Dalton, star of a long-running TV serial. She was noted less for her beauty than for the fact that it had endured remarkably, enabling her in her mid-fifties to play a siren who competed successfully with women half her age. Her greeting was polite, but her

49

green eyes held a kind of amused resentment, as if she found both annoying and absurd someone of my years joining the party.

The other couple were a Mr. and Mrs. Thayer. He was a bald man who looked both rich and bored. She had blond hair the shade of expensive champagne, and a face as wide-eyed and wrinkle-free as a doll's. Almost as expressionless as a doll's, too, even when she smiled. The smile gave an impression of extreme caution, as if she feared her face might crack. To my knowledge, I had never seen anyone with a surgically lifted face, and yet I was sure Mrs. Thayer's had been.

Our host seated me between himself and Elisa Dalton, ordered a glass of white wine for me from the hovering waiter, and then said, "I'm afraid I didn't introduce myself, Miss Hargreaves. I'm Manuelo Covarrubias, Dr. Covarrubias."

A doctor. I would have expected him to be almost anything else—a Bolivian plantation owner, or an Italian nobleman, or a French film star whose pictures had not yet been shown in America—but certainly not a doctor. Then I realized that it might account for that sense of power. Under certain circumstances, a doctor can be as powerful

50

as any man on earth, since his is the power of life or death.

He said, "We were talking about the tennis matches at Hilton Head yesterday. Do you play tennis, Miss Hargreaves?"

"A little."

"Are you a student at the music academy here in San Jimenez?"

"Yes." Then, embarrassed at being in the spotlight before these important people, I said, "I love watching you on TV, Miss Dalton."

"Thank you. Would you like my autograph?"

Taken aback, I said nothing.

"Now, Elisa." Manuelo Covarrubias's voice held amusement and yet a certain edge. "Miss Hargreaves doesn't really look like one of those autograph-hunting kids who swarm around you, does she?"

Her green eyes, holding sparks, looked into his dark ones. I found my voice. "But I would love to have Miss Dalton's autograph."

"You see?" she said to Dr. Covarrubias.

"What I see," he answered, "is that Miss Hargreaves has a tact rare in one of her years."

"Oh, stow it!" she snapped. Reaching into

a tote bag beside her chair, a bag of the same yellow linen as her dress, she brought out a pad of paper and an attached gold pencil. She wrote her name, handed me the slip.

"Thank you, Miss Dalton." I put the slip in the pocket of my beige silk skirt. Or rather, not mine. The Inn's. Along with its matching blouse, it was on loan to me from one of the smart boutiques that adjoined the lobby.

Elisa Dalton, her good humor apparently restored, said, "You're more than welcome."

The bald man returned to the subject of tennis. I stayed with them for about ten minutes, putting in a few words occasionally. Then I spoke my thanks and good-byes and returned to the piano. When I looked around, perhaps twenty minutes later, their table was empty.

My work was finished at seven o'clock, after which a trio took over in the hotel's dining room. I went to the boutique that loaned me my working clothes. Like the hotel's other smart and hideously expensive little shops, it remained open until nine in hope of making sales to the dinner trade. I hung the beige silk in the tiny dressing room permanently assigned to me, dressed in my own stone-washed jeans and blue cotton shirt, and went out into the shop. Miss Garner, the manager, was the only one there. She stood behind a glass-topped case of mohair sweaters, inspecting her nails.

I said, "I met a Dr. Covarrubias today. Do you know anything about him?"

"You kidding? You don't know who he is?"

With her customers Miss Garner used a certain kind of speech, loaded with fashionable exaggerations. Clothes were "smashing" or "too, too divine" or "really sinfully chic." With me she dropped all that.

"Oh, I forgot," she said. "You're not from around here. Still, I'd have thought—Anyway, he's a bigshot plastic surgeon. Runs a kind of sanatorium called Serena, about thirty miles up the valley. Very discreet, very secluded. Well off the highway down a long private road. If you've got the cash, plenty of cash, he'll lift anything for you that sags."

"He seems—very attractive."

"I'll say. First-class catnip. But not for little kitty-cats like you. You'd better stick to your sharps and flats."

"Oh, for heaven's sake! I just remarked that he seemed attractive. I'll probably never see him again."

I was undressing in my room at the academy dorm that night when I heard the phone ring out in the hall. Moments later someone pounded on the door. "Hargreaves! Telephone."

I put on a robe and went out into the hall. "Hello."

"Miss Hargreaves? This is Dr. Covarrubias." He paused briefly. "Do you know where Martinson's restaurant is?"

My pulse quickened. After a moment I said, rather shakily, "Yes."

"Will you have dinner with me there tomorrow night? I could pick you up at your dorm at eight. I won't keep you out late. I know you must have classes the next morning."

"Thank you," I managed to say. "That sounds very nice."

Martinson's was a straightforward sort of place, short on smart decor and long on good food. At one of the white-clothed tables set comfortably far apart in the dark-paneled room we ate broiled lamb chops and crisp fresh green beans.

To my relief, he carried most of the conversational burden, talking of his family's origins in Spain. His father, a count, had been an adherent of Franco's (So I had been right about his aristocratic lineage. I'd just had the wrong country.) A few years after the Spanish Civil War, Manuelo's father and Franco had had a serious falling out. Covarrubias and his wife and his only child at that time, a daughter, had come to the United States, filed for citizenship, and bought a house in Connecticut. Two years later Manuelo Covarrubias had been born.

"When I was halfway through Harvard Medical School, I decided to specialize in plastic surgery. Once I had my license I spent a year in Vietnam, patching up the wounded. After that I practiced in New York for a while, then came out here and started Serena Sanatorium. Perhaps you've heard of it."

"Yes." I didn't add that I had first heard of it only the day before.

"Well," he said, "that's about it."

That certainly was not "it," not for a girl who found herself teetering on the brink of falling in love. There was one question that had to be asked, right away. "Are you married, Dr. Covarrubias?"

"Manuelo. No, I'm not married. If I had been, I'd have contrived to let you know that before I asked you out."

"Haven't you ever been married?"

"Now, isn't that a rather foolish question, Sara? Of course I've been married. After all, I'm forty-three years old." He gave a somewhat wry smile. "Maybe it's a symptom of my being forty-three that I choose to be sitting here with a college girl."

"You were married just once?"

"Twice. In the case of the first wife, I wanted the divorce; in the case of the second, she did." He paused. "Don't you think it's time you told me a little about yourself?"

I told him. My father's death. My mother's struggles to keep us both housed and clothed and fed while putting aside money for a musical education I felt would be wasted on me.

"Are you sure of that? Sure you're not more talented than you realize?"

"I'm sure. So is the academy. Do you think that if I had a future on the concert stage they would have sent me over to play pop music at the Inn?"

"I suppose you're right. Well, it's a sad story, but not an uncommon one. Parents who are quite aware of their own limitations can be wildly optimistic about their children's abilities."

For a while we ate in silence. Then I asked, "Are you on a sort of vacation?"

56

"Yes. I felt I needed to get away from the sanatorium for a few weeks. Incidentally, it's really a hospital too, since we do surgical procedures there, but the patients prefer the term sanatorium. Anyway, I thought of going over to the coast and driving up to the Canadian border. Now, though, I think I'll stay at the Inn for a while longer. It's the best hotel I know, it's got a good tennis pro, and my game could stand improvement."

I kept my gaze fixed on my plate, lest he read in my eyes the hope that it was more than tennis keeping him here. After several moments I looked up and asked, "Does Elisa Dalton play tennis?"

"I don't think so." He smiled. "Anyway, not with me."

"Then you're not a close friend of hers?"

"No. The other thing you want to know about her is whether or not she has been a patient of mine. I'm not betraying any confidence by saying yes. She often tells reporters that she's had a few facial tucks here and there. Even without them, she would be a highly attractive woman. A narcissist, of course. But then, maybe a certain amount of narcissism is as essential to an actress as muscles are to a football lineman."

The waiter removed our plates and handed

us a dessert menu. We both decided to settle for coffee.

At ten-thirty he drove me home through night air that had a fall crispness. Before he had called for me at the dorm, I'd expected that his car would be a two-seater, perhaps a Porsche. Instead it was a BMW sedan. It was impressive, though, with its silent motor, soft seats upholstered in gray leather, and gleaming fruitwood dashboard. He turned on the stereo, punched the button for an all-classical station. The Vivaldi that filled the car was of better tonal quality than most stereo music I had heard in living rooms.

I had not only expected a Porsche. I had expected—hoped?—that he would make a pass. Instead he drove straight to the dormitory, climbed up the steps beside me, then took the hand I extended.

I thanked him, and he said, still holding my hand, "How about dinner next Thursday night?"

"Oh, yes! I mean, I'd like that."

He said good night and went down the steps.

The next weekend I said nothing to my mother about Manuelo. Nor did I mention him the weekend after that, even though his name trembled on my lips a dozen times.

Because by then I was hopelessly, helplessly in love. Before that I had thought I was in love. There'd been a boy with whom I'd gone steady during all my junior year and part of my senior year in high school. Later, for about three weeks, until we'd had a violent political argument, I had thought I was falling in love with a faculty member at the academy—a twenty-seven-year-old musicology teacher. But I had never experienced anything like the intensity of my emotion for Manuelo Covarrubias. I daydreamed through my classes and my hours of piano practice. The only times that seemed real to me were when Manuelo and I sat across a restaurant table from each other, or when at the Inn he walked into the cocktail lounge, sometimes with the Thayers or other guests, more often alone.

The maddening part was that he did not try to make love to me. I knew he wanted to. The look in his eyes told me so, again and again. So did the tone of his voice. And yet he didn't so much as kiss me good night. Why? Why?

At Martinson's one night, almost three weeks after we had met, he said abruptly, "I'm going back to Serena tomorrow."

Holding a fork filled with mashed potatoes, I died a little.

"I want you to come there, as soon as possible."

I came back to life. "You want me to come to Serena? Why?"

"To work for me. I'll want you to play for my patients while they have their cocktails —alcoholic or non-alcoholic as the case may be—and later on at dinner. I think you're just right for the job. You're pretty, and fairly well poised, and yet there's something diffident about you. You're not one of those terrifying self-assured nineteen-year-olds."

"Leave the academy?" I said.

"Why not? You said you were wasting your time and both your mother's and your money here. If things don't work out at the sanatorium, you can always leave and enroll in another college. I'll pay you twice what you're making here, so you'll be saving plenty—that is, if you can stay out of the Serena boutique with its eight-hundred-dollar alligator belts and twenty-five-hundred-dollar handbags. Well, how about it?"

Did he want me there just as a pianist? Of course not, I told myself with a flood of joy and yearning. Once I was there, he would

60

give way to his own desire, a desire I could see in his dark eyes right at that moment.

"Yes," I said.

The next weekend, of course, I did have to tell my mother about Manuelo. In the living room of the little apartment above the hardware store, which she continued to occupy in the wintertime, I said, "Mother, I'm leaving the academy."

After a moment she said in a stunned voice, "Leaving?"

"Yes. I've been offered a wonderful job playing the piano at Serena. That's a sanatorium about thirty miles north of San Jimenez. That means it's thirty miles closer to Oresburg." I knew that would not be of much comfort, but it was the best I had to offer her.

She said, still in that sleep-walking voice, "Sanatorium?"

"The people there aren't sick. It's for plastic surgery cases. Rich women, mostly, some of them famous. The pay is wonderful, twice what I'm getting at the Miraflores Inn."

The stunned look was clearing from her face. My mother never had much education, but she was far from stupid. Now she went right to the point.

"Who offered you this job?"

"A Dr. Covarrubias."

"Who is he?"

"A plastic surgeon. He started the sanatorium."

"What is he like?"

I might as well be frank, I thought. After all, she would realize the situation as soon as she saw us together. And that would be soon. Manuelo had said she would be welcome to visit me at the sanatorium.

"Oh, Mother! He's the most attractive man I ever met, the most attractive man I ever even saw."

Again she went straight to the point. "He must be years older than you."

"He's forty-three."

"Forty-three. A year older than I am. A year younger than your father would have been if he had lived."

"Mother! He's not like other people." Neither were Elisa Dalton or Mrs. Thayer, I reflected fleetingly. If people had enough money and determination, apparently they could hold time at bay. "He's handsome, he can play three sets of tennis without breathing hard—Oh, Mother! You just won't understand until you meet him."

In an almost toneless voice she said, "I

understand that you're in love with him. How does he feel about you?"

"He loves me! I know he does, even though he hasn't said so. Please, Mother! I'm not a child. If—if I'm wrong about him, if things don't work out, I can always leave."

"And then what? Perhaps the academy won't take you back."

"The academy! Oh, Mother! Isn't there any way I can convince you that I'm just wasting time and money there?"

We argued for about half an hour. Then she must have realized that she had no chance of winning that old argument, now that I was in love with Manuelo.

She looked at me with eyes emptied of that long-held dream, the dream of me seated at a grand piano on a concert stage. Only her love and her fear for me remained in her eyes.

"All right, Sara. As you say, you are no longer a child. Go to this Serena place. All I can do is pray that you are going to be happy."

Now, as I sat with Mike Rolfe in his one-room-kitchenette apartment, Beethoven's *Emperor* Concerto came to its triumphant close. The silence that followed was broken by the ring of the desk bell in the motel office. He went out to answer it. When he returned he said, "Trucker with a load of machine tools for San Diego." He sat down beside me and lifted the brandy bottle. "A little more?"

"No, thanks. I have to report to Sammy's at six, remember? Tell me, how could I get to a shopping mall from here? Without a car, I mean."

"Walk two blocks north. There's a bus line. The bus doesn't run very often—you know what public transportation is like in southern California—but it'll take you straight to the biggest shopping mall in town."

"Thank you." I looked at my watch. "A quarter past ten. I'd better get to sleep."

"I'll walk you up to your room."

We went outside. The parking lot was almost full of trucks and passenger cars, but no sound except an occasional snore came from behind the motel room doors. As Mike had said, his was a sober and hard-working clientele, at least on weeknights. Overhead, bright February stars were visible despite the city's lights and the yellow glow of the parking lot arc lamps.

He unlocked my door, pushed it back, and gave me the key. "Good night, Sara."

"Good night. It was an awfully good dinner, Mike."

"Wait until you taste my spareribs. Oh, another thing. Arnie will come on duty soon." Arnie, I gathered, was the sleepy-looking youth I had glimpsed in the motel office that morning. "I'll tell him to give you a ring at five-fifteen. That ought to leave you enough time to get to Sammy's by six."

He bent his tall, thin frame, placed a brief, brotherly kiss on my cheek, and walked away.

5

I did not sleep well. That wasn't surprising. For one thing, there were all those hours and hours I had slept the previous afternoon and night. For another, certain memories of Manuelo, never far below the surface of my thoughts, had come into full consciousness. Nights in his big bed in that luxurious apartment at Serena. And that final, terrible memory of him . . .

The last time I'd looked at the luminous dial of my motel room clock the hands had pointed to almost one. I'd slept soon after

65

that, and awakened in darkness a few minutes before Arnie called me on the phone.

Over at Sammy's I changed into my uniform, ate a breakfast of canned orange juice and packaged corn flakes—no toast—and then went on duty. As on the day before, I found the work dull but undemanding. The customers, from truck drivers to large Mexican families to the old folks, were all polite. And considering that this was a fast-food joint, the tips were generous.

After two o'clock I sat down for my belated lunch. I decided to try the "generous slice of country-cured ham, accompanied by luscious golden pineapple." The pineapple was all right. There's not much you can do to ruin canned pineapple, as long as you keep it refrigerated after the can is opened. But the ham slice, thin and slightly burned, with its fatty edges curled, tasted as I imagine the boiled shoe leather might have to Charlie Chaplin in that old silent classic.

During my period of employment at Sammy's—it was part of a chain, I learned —I was to become more and more convinced about the perverted genius guiding its culinary destiny. Almost everything I tried was terrible.

The strange part was that I never heard

anyone complain, not even the senior citizens. From their flat Middle Western accents, I concluded that most of them had formed their food tastes while growing up on farms in states like Ohio or Indiana. But either down-home cooking was not as good as legend tells us, or these people had come to accept Sammy's food as they accepted other trials afflicting people their age, like rheumatism and errant social security checks.

Eventually I was to find something edible on the menu—a tuna salad sandwich. The bread, whether whole wheat or white, was always too soft, and the mayonnaise had been thinned until it dripped, but the flavor wasn't too bad.

That second day of my employment at Sammy's, though, I paid for my half-price burned ham and then set out for the bus stop. Two blocks from the highway I knew I had reached the right corner because there sat a bench with LOS CERRITOS BUS LINES painted on its backrest. I looked up the street. No bus in sight. After a moment's hesitation I continued in the same direction. The street where I had left the Tattinger Institute car was only two blocks away. I hurried on, the sole pedestrian on a sidewalk that led past small, neat houses and lawns set with dwarf palms, rubber trees, and riotously blooming subtropical shrubs. At the second corner I looked to my left.

The gray Chevrolet was still there, parked in front of the vacant lot. Plainly, no cruising patrol car had investigated it. No householder had inquired if one of his neighbors owned the car, or notified the police.

I turned swiftly and retraced my steps, over sidewalks that remained so empty that I recalled stories about people who had been stopped by suspicious police merely because they were walking rather than driving.

I sat down on the vacant bench. When the bus finally came, it held the sort of passengers you might expect—two giggly girls of about fourteen, a palsied woman of perhaps eighty, and a scowling young man whose splinted and bandaged right leg explained why he, unlike most other first-class California citizens, was not behind the wheel of a car.

Once aboard, I arrived at the shopping mall in a remarkably short time. And there I found luck was with me; the stores were having their February sales. I bought several separates—another pair of white duck pants, a bright yellow cotton skirt, and two white cotton blouses and a white T-shirt.

I had less good fortune in the mall's one luggage store. No sale items there. Even a canvas carryall was out of my financial reach.

"Do you know where I might find secondhand luggage?"

"Secondhand!" From the salesman's expression one might have thought I had inquired about buying a sack of cow manure. "The only secondhand stores I know of around here are antique shops. But I'm sure there are plenty of such stores in the Mexican part of town."

"How can I get there? I don't have a car. I came here by bus."

Now his expression said that he found me a very strange person indeed. "Which direction did your bus come from?"

"East, I think."

"Then just take the same bus back and stay on it until you get to Old Town. Tell the driver to let you off there."

When I got to Old Town I liked it. The little frame and stucco houses were bright with pink and blue and green paint. Flowers —some real, some plastic—filled the tiny front yards. Tape players in open-fronted cantinas blared salsa and mariachi music into the street. No empty sidewalks *here*. Children with gleeful laughs and big dark eyes played everywhere. Ample women in bright blouses and skintight stretch pants stood in chattering groups. Parked at the curbs were the sort of large but battered old sedans that I had heard a waitress at Sammy's refer to contemptuously as "bean wagons."

I had no trouble finding a suitcase. On a two-block stretch there were a half-dozen secondhand stores, selling everything from clothing to cooking utensils. Outside one of them I spotted an only-slightly-scratched blue suitcase of some sort of plastic material. The price? Four dollars. I put my small purchases in the suitcase and started back toward the bus stop.

A delicious aroma of boiling beans assailed my nostrils. I stopped before the sidewalk counter of an open-fronted cafe, where a massive woman was stirring the contents of a big iron pot. She beamed at me, took a white plastic spoon from a cupful of multi-colored ones on the counter, and dipped the spoon into the pot. "Taste," she said.

The brown beans were delicious, mealy in texture, and not overly flavored. She said, "You buy, no?"

I could scarcely hope for another dinner invitation from Mike so soon. That meant I would have to eat at Sammy's or at some other nearby place, which might or might not be any better. But with these beans, plus a green pepper and some fruit I had seen at a stand a few yards away—

"I don't have a stove," I said.

She understood. "I show you how to keep hot." She took a pint-size paper carton down from a shelf above the stove. "You want this much?"

I nodded.

She filled the container, placed it inside a paper bag lined with aluminum foil, added one of the plastic spoons from the counter, and closed the outer bag.

Carrying my suitcase and my carton of beans, I walked to the vegetable stall, then to the bus stop. When I reached my motel room I saw with relief that the workmen had gone for the day.

A moment after I entered the room my phone rang. "Find the mall okay?" Mike asked.

"Yes. Then I went sightseeing in Old Town." I didn't say anything about the suitcase, of course. "I bought some boiled beans."

"Good. Bring them down here. Mexican *frijoles* should go fine with my barbecued ribs. That is, if you're free for dinner tonight."

"I think I can fit it into my social calendar."

"Can you make it around six?"

"Sure."

"See you then."

When we'd hung up I looked at my watch. Almost five. Several channels would have local news broadcasts. With fingers that were not quite steady, I turned the set on.

A young black woman bade me good evening and then said, "At this hour Sara Hargreaves, known as the young Jean Harris, is still at large. Convicted almost four years ago of killing her plastic surgeon lover in a jealous rage, Miss Hargreaves escaped three days ago from Tattinger Institute, the women's prison southeast of Los Angeles. Police announce they have several leads.

"A three-car accident on the Coast Highway early this morning held up traffic for—"

I snapped the set off. What leads, I wondered, my heart pounding. Or were there any leads? Probably not. It was just what "police spokesmen" were always saying, along with something about expecting to make an arrest "shortly." After all, they hadn't even found that car.

Or had they? Were they watching it from one of the houses along that street, hoping that I would return to it and try to drive off? No, surely they must not think me that stupid. When and if they found the Chevy, they would think that I had gone to ground somewhere nearby, or had left Los Cerritos by intercity bus, the Amtrak train, or still another stolen car.

And Mike. Had he been watching news broadcasts? He must have. Everybody did. But why should I fear that he would connect the girl I could now see in the mirror—brown eyes, sleek cap of brown hair—with that four-year-old photograph broadcast on TV?

Still, any relationship with him would be risky. Last night I had gotten by with saying almost nothing about myself. Our few hours together had been filled with Beethoven, the frequent ringing of the motel's desk bell, and Mike's talk about himself. But sooner or later, I would have to offer him more information.

Of course, I could stop seeing him. I could pack everything in that secondhand suitcase and walk away from this motel room and my job at Sammy's right now. But where would I go? And the more job applications I made, the more room registration cards I filled out, the more chance I would betray myself by one response or another.

And an abrupt disappearance might set Mike to thinking—hard. He might decide that it was his duty to inform the police, lest there be some connection between Sara Hargreaves and the other Sara who had showed up at his motel, carless, a few hours after Sara Hargreaves had driven away in a prison Chevrolet.

No. Best to stay on here, improvising as each difficulty or danger came up, rather like an Eliza crossing the ice by leaping from one floe to another.

Right now there was the problem of what I should say in answer to his almost inevitable questions. I regretted that I had written "San Jimenez" on my motel registration card. Of course, I could not have entered as a home address either Oresburg or that little town near the Serena sanatorium. But I must be careful not even to mention the San Jimenez Academy of Music. After my arrest the reporters had frequently, though erroneously, referred to me as a "talented pianist."

Fortunately the city of San Jimenez had another institution of higher learning, a teachers' college. I could tell Mike that I was currently enrolled there, but had had a falling out with a young man I had considered marrying and so had needed to get away to think things through. I could add that I just didn't feel like talking about it. Except for the surliness he manifested about every aspect of his present occupation, Mike seemed well-mannered enough. He wouldn't press me to talk about it.

I opened my secondhand suitcase and took out my new yellow cotton skirt.

6

That evening my story about the teachers' college and my troubles with my fiancé seemed to work. At least Mike did not ask for any details.

For the next ten days or so I continued to work the early-morning shift at Sammy's, eat my half-priced lunches, and then go to my room, where I would use my radio or

TV to help drown out the sounds of plastering, hammering, and heavy-metal music.

Some evenings I returned to Sammy's for a tuna sandwich dinner. ("You must be just nuts about tuna," one of the other waitresses said to me.) Other nights I accepted Mike's invitations to share his evening meal. Twice I ventured down the narrow sidewalk between the crowded highway and the new- and used-car lots to another fast-food place called Sue Ann's. The food there wasn't great, but it was better than my employer's.

As I moved along the sidewalk during these short excursions from the motel, I threw swift glances into the used-car lots. Here and there were cars that appeared to be ten years old or even more. Veritable "bean wagons," yes, but the prices posted on the windshields were within my range, and the cars looked as if they would get me as far as Oresburg when I decided the time was ripe to go there.

During that strange interval, when my life centered around the motel and Sammy's, I thought more about the past than I ever had while at Tattinger. In prison I had lived from day to day as if in some long, dull dream, with little thought of either the past or the future. Perhaps that was the way prisoners instinctively tried to cope with their situation. Several of my fellow inmates confided to me that they too felt that they were in a kind of waking dream.

But now that I was at least temporarily free, memories poured in on me as I served hamburgers and fries, or lay awake at night in my room. For some reason, I recalled most frequently the day of my arrival at Serena Sanatorium.

Manuelo had met me at the highway bus stop—just a roofed bench—one late November afternoon and then driven me in the BMW along the narrow dirt road that led through low, rolling hills to the sanatorium. In the distance the Sierra Nevada, crests glimmering with snow, looked tall against the darkening sky.

Somehow I had expected Serena to be of Spanish architecture, all cream-colored stucco and red tile. Instead it was a rambling, three-story structure of redwood. Although Manuelo had built it only eight years before, he had patterned it after turn-of-the-century resort hotels at Lake Tahoe and Yosemite.

We left the car at the foot of the broad front steps, climbed them to a long veranda, and then entered a wide central hall, its highly polished floor reflecting the glow of lights set in wall brackets. Ahead, a staircase soared upward. Through a wide doorway to the right I could see a huge living room. Oriental rugs, lots of chintz in draperies and slipcovers. The old-money look. A few women sat in small groups on the oversized sofas and wingback armchairs. All of them, even one with a bandaged neck, gave me an impression of opulence and chic.

A little farther on, to the left, was the big dining room. Two women in blue cotton uniforms moved about between tables for four, laying flat silver on placemats. "The first floor," Manuelo said, "holds the common rooms—salon, dining room, boutique, game room, and so on—with servants' quarters at the rear. The second floor is the sanatorium proper, with the operating room and the patients' rooms. The third floor is for resident staff and for guests. It's also for patients who decide for one reason or another to stay on even after there is no medical reason for them not to leave. You'll be on that floor."

A little way beyond the foot of the stairs he maneuvered himself and me and my two suitcases into a small mahogany-paneled elevator. A moment later I glimpsed through its grilled doors a broad linoleum-floored hallway, along which a white-clad male attendant was pushing an empty gurney. Then the elevator stopped at the third floor.

We stepped out into a hall carpeted in deep brown pile. Oil landscapes, each with an attached tubular light, lined the dark paneled walls. Beside a door opposite the elevator Manuelo set down my suitcase. Then, he opened the door and stood aside for me to enter.

"This is my apartment."

Again the statement was old money, but masculine this time. Black leather sofa and armchair, hunting prints on the walls, and, above the fireplace, a beautiful oil painting of a bay horse. The artist, Manuelo said, was an eighteenth-century painter named Stubbs. There were other masculine touches, too—ancient-looking rifles crossed on one wall, and, on a refectory table a glass-topped case of knives with blades about eight inches long and ivory handles incised with a zigzag pattern.

Manuelo saw me looking at them. "African hunting knives," he said, "from Nigeria."

"Are you a weapons collector?"

He laughed. "Lord, no. The knives and the flintlocks were the decorator's idea. He was going in heavily for macho that season."

"So that was it," I said. Through a half-open door in the far wall I could see a king-size bed and part of a bureau. Manuelo's bed, I thought.

"I've ordered our dinner brought up here," he said, and nodded toward something I had not noticed before. Near the fireplace was the entrance to a little balcony, glass-enclosed against the winter coolness, and set with a glass-topped table of black wrought iron and two wrought-iron chairs. "And now I'll show you to your room."

Carrying my suitcases, he led me down the hall toward the front of the building. At the hall's end twilight showed through a long window. He stopped at the last door on our right and opened it.

I stepped past him into a room which was as feminine as his apartment was masculine. Blue wallpaper with a tiny white flower. Braided rugs on the gleaming hardwood floor. A puffy blue coverlet on the bed. A chaise longue covered in flowered chintz, and a dressing table with a skirt that matched. There was a small fireplace with a white marble mantel and, near it, an armoire with doors deeply carved in a grapeleaf design. The armoire looked old and valuable.

At one end of the room, through a half-open door, I could see part of a bathroom.

I moved to the windows. Enough daylight remained to show me that the front window overlooked the broad lawn set with outdoor chairs and umbrella-topped tables. From the side window I could look down into a garden set with blossom-laden rosebushes and, on pedestals, mirrored balls that gleamed dimly. Directly below the window was a cement basin, evidently a fishpond that had been drained in anticipation of the brief California winter.

"Oh, it's all so lovely."

"Women usually like this room," he said.

I felt a stab of jealousy. "Women?"

He nodded. "When I started this place, the housekeeper had this room. Then she moved to one at the back. Since then, released patients who don't want to leave have occupied this room. The last such person was a Danish princess who stayed on for more than a month. She weighed more than two hundred pounds, but she was a genuine princess."

He started toward the bathroom doorway. "I told Mrs. Guerrero—Yes, she gave you lots of towels." He turned back to me. "Maria Guerrero is the housekeeper. She's known me for longer than I can remember. I was only two years old when she came to work for my family as a domestic." He looked at his watch. "Will it be all right with you if we have dinner at eight o'clock?"

It was marvelous, eating swordfish and steamed broccoli on that little balcony opening off his living room. An almost full moon had risen. He had dimmed the lights in the living room, so that the main illumination was that flood of blue-white moonlight and the glow of candles on the small table, their wavering flames reflected in the balcony's glass walls.

"Everything is so—so—" My voice trailed off.

"It's even nicer out here in the summer. You'll see."

Summer. The future, our future together, stretching ahead of us. My heart swelled with a half-incredulous happiness. How was it that I, neither brilliant nor talented, and only attractive rather than beautiful, should be sitting here with Manuelo Covarrubias?

It was during our simple fruit dessert that the woman came in. She just opened the hall door and came across the room to the balcony—a tall, thin woman in an expensive suit of wool knit, her dark hair drawn back into a chignon. Oversized black glasses hid at least half her face, and I could see reflections of the candle flames dancing in them. Below the glasses her mouth was bitter.

Manuelo had gotten to his feet. I could sense that he was very angry, but the only outward sign of it was a muscle jumping along his jawline. "Good evening, Paula." He paused. "Shouldn't you have knocked first?"

"If I had, would you have let me in?"

"No." Then, "If you really have something to say to me, Paula—and you don't, you know—come to my office tomorrow morning. I told you that the last time you came barging in here."

The face with the masking glasses turned to me, then back to him. "And tonight I'm even less welcome, right?"

"Right."

"So. It was to be a memorable evening. Well, maybe I can make it even more memorable for your young friend, your *very* young friend."

She turned her face toward me and whipped off the glasses. With an indrawn breath, I shrank against the back of my chair. I saw dark, hating eyes, the left one half hidden by a drooping lid, set in a mass of scar tissue.

"Paula! Put on your glasses!"

Slowly, and with a one-sided smile, as if to indicate that she was doing so only because she chose to, she put on the black glasses.

Manuelo's voice shook ever so slightly. "What happened to you was tragic, but it was not my fault. It was a result of your own impatience and bad judgment. Lawyers have told you that, and other doctors, and you own husband. Now will you please leave?"

Her hand shot out and grasped the stem of his filled wine glass. He seized her wrist. "Please, Paula. No melodrama. Now put down that glass. I don't want to use force, but if I have to, I'll march you to the elevator."

For a moment they faced each other. I could imagine the expression in the eyes behind the glasses. Then he relaxed his grip. She set down the wine glass, crossed to the door, and closed it behind her.

Manuelo sank into his chair. I said nothing whatever.

After perhaps a minute he said, "Her name is Paula Winship. She's the wife of an airplane manufacturer. She came to me for an ordinary eye job, upper and lower lids.

84

Everything went well. Then, days before I was ready to release her from the sanatorium, she said she was going home. She'd gotten the notion—she's a little paranoid, I've learned—that it was really her husband's idea rather than hers that had brought her here for the eye job. He wanted to be free, she had concluded, for a little fling. I protested, but she said she would hire a nurse trained in plastic surgical procedures, to stay with her until it was time to remove the bandages. I did the only thing I could do—made her sign a release and then let her go.

"After she got home, she not only took off the bandages too soon. She also tore some of the stitches. Still, everything might have been all right if she had come back to me. But maybe she was too embarrassed to do that. Anyway, she went to this surgeon who hadn't been much good even before he got hooked on cocaine. He did to her what you saw tonight. She sued the other doctor, of course, but before the case could come to trial he died of a drug overdose. She knows she has no case against me, but evidently it brings her some sort of satisfaction to turn up here every once in a while."

"Does she—bother the other patients?"

"You mean, tell them I did that to her? No. She knows it would be of no use. The small circle of women who can afford places like Serena know all about what happened to Paula Winship. Oh, Sara! I'm so sorry she came here and ruined—"

"She didn't!" I cried fiercely. "She didn't ruin anything."

He smiled at me. "That's my Sara."

He filled my wine glass and his own. We sat there. Gradually the world seemed to narrow down to nothing but mingled moonlight and candleglow, and the man across the table from me.

"Sara?"

I looked into the handsome face with its unsmiling lips, its questioning eyes. "Yes," I said.

He stood up, reached his hand down to me. I took it. Together we walked into the bedroom. By the refracted glow of the dim living room lights he took me in his arms and kissed me. Perhaps it was because of long denial that I found that first kiss so dizzying, a kind of sweet shock that went through me down to my toes.

He said, in a constricted voice, "I want to undress you."

I nodded.

He undressed me slowly, fingers lingering over the buttons of my blouse, the hooks of my bra, the elastic waist of my panties. Then I waited on the bed while he undressed and lay down beside me. Our lovemaking was everything, and more, that I had fantasized as I played for cocktail guests at the Miraflores Inn, or tossed in my bed in the music academy dorm at night.

When we finally lay quiet, my head pillowed on his arm, I asked, "Why, Manuelo?"

"Why what?" His voice sounded lazy.

"Why did you wait so long to make love to me?"

He smiled up into the dimness. "If all I had wanted was a one-night stand, I wouldn't have waited. But I wanted more than that. I held off so that you would want me, want me enough that there'd not be much chance that you would slip away from me afterwards."

As I looked at that smile of his, the chilling word "technique" flashed through my mind. One technique for one-night stands, another for girls he thought he might want for a long time. How long? Several weeks? Months?

I thrust the thought away. "Manuelo, do you love me?"

"Of course."

"You haven't said so. You haven't said so even tonight."

"I hadn't thought it needed saying. But I do love you."

I drew a deep breath. "Will we get married?" I had to ask it to try to keep that ugly word "technique" at bay.

He smoothed my hair back from my face. "I think so. But I'm a two-time loser, Sara. I want to be very sure this time. I want us both to be. Do you understand?"

I was sure already. And in time I would make him sure, so much so that he would wonder how he had ever gotten along without me.

My arm tightened over his bare chest. "Yes, I understand."

We made love again, more slowly this time. Then he said, "I told Mrs. Guerrero to have your breakfast brought to your room in the mornings. I think it would be best for the maid to find you there."

I roused myself from a delicious languor. "Then I'd better leave now."

I got up, dressed. In a terrycloth robe Manuelo accompanied me to the doorway of his apartment. He waited there until I turned to call a soft good night from the doorway of my own room.

7

A light knocking on my door brought me awake. I sat up in bed, looked around the sun-flooded room for a disoriented moment, and then called, "Who is it, please?" If it was Manuelo, I would say, "Just a minute," and then dash to the bathroom for a hurried hair comb.

"It's the housekeeper, Mrs. Guerrero."

I looked at my watch. Eight-thirty. "Come in, please."

The door opened, and a tall woman in a subdued print dress of black and beige walked in, a tray in her hands. Her face, framed in graying dark hair, was dignified, even haughty. And although she must have been well into her sixties, her erect carriage matched her face.

She said, "I'm short-handed this morning." Despite her Hispanic name, she had no trace of accent, and so probably she had been born in this country. "That's why I'm bringing your breakfast."

89

And perhaps because she was curious to see me? "Thank you very much."

"Shall I put it across your lap?"

"Why not here on the table beside the bed?"

She put the tray down. A rich coffee aroma steamed from a little silver pot. Beside it was a bowl of strawberries and a white china cream pitcher. There was also a covered silver dish. I lifted its lid and saw tiny sausages and scrambled eggs. A breakfast fit for a queen, one in training for the Olympics.

"Oh, my!" I said.

I looked up to see an amused shine, faintly touched with scorn, in her dark eyes. I could imagine her thinking, "You're far from the first one to catch his eye."

Maybe so, I thought. But if I have anything to say about it, I'll be the last. Then, just to prove that her expression had not disconcerted me, I asked, "Has Dr. Covarrubias had breakfast yet?"

"Of course. He's up at six every morning and has breakfast with his staff on the second floor." She paused, and then went on, "That's the way he keeps hands-on management. It's one of the reasons Serena is the best sanatorium of its kind in the country."

The proprietary pride in her voice was so pronounced that for a moment I was startled. Then I remembered what Manuelo had told me. Because she had come to work for his parents when he was still an infant, she had known him practically all his life.

"Oh," she said, reaching into her pocket, "here is a note he sent you."

"Thank you." I laid the envelope, unopened, beside my breakfast tray.

"Anything else you need?"

"No, thank you, Mrs. Guerrero."

She left the room. Before I dove into that sumptuous breakfast, I opened his note:

My darling,

Perhaps I forgot to tell you that you'll have your lunches, buffet style, in the first floor dining room. I take all my daytime meals with the staff. But tonight around eight, right after you have finished your dinnertime stint at the piano? The two of us up here, same as last night?

With a sense that the whole world was mine, I poured an amber stream of coffee into my cup.

After breakfast I left my room to go exploring. Through the grill of the elevator door I could see that the car was not on my floor. Instead of pushing the button, I descended the back staircase two flights and pushed open a baize door into the ground-floor hall. I encountered no one there, and the only person I saw in the big salon was a maid pushing a vacuum cleaner over one of the Oriental rugs.

Out on the broad lawn, though, several women were seated in thickly padded redwood chairs. Eager to be alone with my happiness on this beautiful day, I merely glanced at them and then went on down the gravel drive to the twin stone pillars that flanked the entrance to the sanatorium grounds.

The winter rains had not started yet. Beyond Serena's green lawns, the rounded, oak-studded hills were tawny as a lion's skin. I left the dirt road beyond the pillars for a narrow path that wandered up a hillside. I stopped beside a live oak around whose trunk someone had built a wooden bench. Seated there, I could look over the sanatorium's low stone wall to the women seated on the lawn, and to the sprawling redwood building itself.

"Stole it from me, he did," said a voice

beside me, suddenly. "Stole it while I was flat on my back and helpless."

My head jerked around. An elderly man stood beside me. In woolen trousers and a checked sports jacket, with a suede leather vest and a suede cap, he looked like an Englishman out for a day's shooting on the moors. It seemed strange to hear him speak with an American accent.

I said, "I'm afraid I don't—"

"Name's Murray, Patrick Murray. I own the land we're on right now, young lady, and I used to own that land down there. All of it was Murray land for more than a hundred fifty years. My great-grandfather bought it from a don, one of the holders of the old Spanish land grants."

"You said something about stealing—"

"It happened while I was in the hospital in Santa Barbara. I knew I'd be there some time so I gave my nephew power of attorney. He's a lawyer as well as my heir, so I trusted him to do the proper thing. Instead, what did he do? Sold thirty acres of my land to a fancy doctor who'd made a fortune getting rid of women's wrinkles."

I felt my temper rising. "You said stole! If your nephew sold it, and at a fair price—"

"Oh, I suppose the price was all right. But

listen to me, young woman! Some men feel that their land should be inviolate, like—like the chastity of their wives."

My indignation abated. It seemed to me that I could look back beyond this well-dressed old man to a long line of Irish peasants, fiercely hungry for land, and, if they somehow got it, fiercely determined to hold onto it.

He asked suddenly, "You're not one of the patients from down there, are you?" Leaning closer, he studied my face with faded blue eyes. "No, I can see you wouldn't be."

"I'm not, but I work there." Before he could ask what sort of work I did, I got to my feet. "Good-bye, Mr. Murray. I think I'll go on with my walk now."

Aware of his following gaze, I climbed to the crest of the low hill and descended to a little valley on the other side.

It was past two when I returned to the sanatorium. No one was in the dining room. I helped myself to cold ham, potato salad, and beans vinaigrette from the buffet table. When I'd eaten, I went to my room. There I changed from duck pants and a green turtleneck to one of the outfits—pink silk shirt and pink silk-and-cotton pants—that Manuelo had selected for me in San Jimenez. It was still an hour before I was scheduled to play for cocktail drinkers in the salon, but I figured I might as well try out the piano ahead of time.

I found the salon empty. In one corner of the big room a grand piano gleamed in the sunlight that slanted through Venetian blinds. I walked to the instrument, started to turn back the keyboard lid, and then stopped, arrested by the sound of a name I knew.

A woman said, "I hear Elisa Dalton may be coming here for a few days." She had a slight lisp. "Not to have any more work done. Just for a rest."

Elisa Dalton—the TV star to whom Manuelo had introduced me at the Miraflores Inn.

I looked out through the slats of the venetian blinds. Two women were out there on a flagstone terrace. Backs turned to me, they sat in peacock rattan chairs that looked like something out of *Casablanca*.

"Coming for a rest! Everyone knows Elisa has had a letch for Manuelo for years—as who, for that matter, hasn't?"

The woman with the lisp said, "I haven't."

"Now, Sally! I'm just about your oldest friend. Don't try to fool me." She paused, but when there was no reply she went on, "I hear that young husband of hers is as jealous as ever."

There had been no husband with her, young or otherwise, at the Inn. Nor had Manuelo mentioned that she was married.

"Yes, and isn't *that* a hoot! When she married him everybody gave it six months at most. After that, they said, he'd be demanding a big settlement to get out of her life, and she'd be glad to pay it."

"Instead, two years later he's still glaring at anyone who looks at her, and moping around like a lost dog whenever she manages to give him the slip."

Was that what she had been doing in San Jimenez, giving her jealous young husband the slip?

"His trouble is a mother complex."

"Whatever it is, I wouldn't mind meeting a man his age who has it."

I couldn't use the piano now. They would be almost certain to realize that they had been overheard. I was about to turn away when I heard the woman with the lisp say, "What is the new one like, the pianist?"

"Different, I hear. For the last few years some of Manuelo's girls, no matter how young, have had 'hooker' written all over them. This one's supposed to be quite nice, and fairly bright. When Manuelo found her, she was enrolled in some sort of musical academy.

"Sounds as if this one might last for a while."

Might, I thought furiously. They could bet their little Ferragamo boots that I would last.

"Well, we'll soon see what she's like. Oh, look at the time! We'd better change."

Swiftly I left the salon and went upstairs. I didn't come down until it was time for me to start playing.

The piano sounded fine. Whether I was playing Porter or Gershwin or Sondheim, the fifteen or so women in the room did not stop chattering. Frequently, though, they gave me a smattering of applause. A few of them came up to request numbers. I sensed that they also wanted a better look at me.

The two women who had been out on the side terrace sat close enough to the piano that I recognized their voices. The one with the lisp was a plump blonde of indeterminate age. Like several of the women in the room, she wore dark glasses, evidently hiding an eye job. Her companion also was blond, but svelte. Unlike most of the women, she wore neither dark glasses nor a bandage—either around her neck or encircling the top of her head and chin. Evidently she was one of those who lingered on after there was no medical reason for them to stay. Unless whatever part of her had been smoothed out, flattened, or lifted was hidden by her gray silk sheath.

At a quarter of six I took a break, moving out onto the deserted side terrace to sit for a while in the gathering dark. Then I went into the dining room to play. As Manuelo had suggested, I gave them light classics, mostly Strauss and Brahms, to accompany their low-calorie meals served on white porcelain. Manuelo had told me that Serena encouraged early bedtimes, and so I wasn't surprised to find the dining room empty by a quarter of eight. Happily I sped up to the third floor.

Hours later, as I lay with my head resting on Manuelo's bare shoulder, he said in his lazy, after-lovemaking voice, "So my ladies seemed to like you."

98

"Yes. At least they were very nice to me."

"They'd better be. I can get plenty of patients, but there is only one you. What did you do today besides play the piano?"

"I went for a walk. And I met a man who said his name was Patrick Murray. He also said he used to own all this land, the land where the sanatorium is." I hesitated, and then went on. "He says you bought it while he was in the hospital."

"So I did. I bought it from his nephew at a fair price. It had to be a fair price. His nephew is a lawyer and a sharp one. But poor old Mr. Murray refuses to see it that way."

"He didn't look poor to me. He had a wristwatch that must have cost thousands."

"I was speaking metaphorically. Anybody is poor who can't stop dwelling on something that's over and done with."

"Where does he live?"

"A couple of miles from here, in the ancestral Murray manse, or rather, in the carriage house behind it." He turned his head and kissed my forehead. "But I can think of more pleasant ways to spend our time than discussing Patrick Murray."

8

At Serena the fall days passed, crisp and sunny except for the occasional morning fog that managed to creep in from the Pacific several miles away. Besides playing for cocktails and dinner, I spent part of each day wandering through the low, oak-studded hills, always alone. Although the patients seemed to like me and my playing well enough, there was a distance between me and these rich, pampered women that neither they nor I tried to bridge.

Sometimes I encountered Patrick Murray during my rambles. Once I'd told him of my job at Serena, he made no further mention of his grievance. Instead he talked of his collection of Civil War histories, or told me Irish jokes, all antiseptically clean, which had been passed down to him by his grandfather.

Once I walked with him to the house his grandfather had built back in the middle of the last century. With its Victorian turrets and bulging bay windows, it looked like something that had wandered out here from an eastern city and been unable to find its way home. It was also considerably run down, its paint peeling and one of its bay windows cracked. That, he told me, was because he no longer lived in the house. "No house for one person to be rolling around in, a huge place like that." Instead, for the past several years he had lived in the remodeled carriage house behind the old mansion. He showed it to me. It was an incongruous sort of place. Pieces of fine mahogany furniture from the big house contrasted with the rough plank flooring, the open loft where Murray slept, and the little lean-to kitchen where he brewed us some tea before we resumed our walk.

Manuelo had said I could use one of the several cars parked in the sprawling garage behind the sanatorium. Thus, a few times I drove up the narrow dirt road and then turned onto the highway toward Milano, eight miles away. The town had been founded in the last century by homesick Italian immigrants who had planted vineyards. These had not flourished, but now, belatedly, the town had. An electronics firm with a fat government contract had built a plant there, and, to accommodate its employees, mobile home parks had sprung up, with shops and restaurants, too.

But what I looked forward to each day, of course, were the hours I would spend with Manuelo in his apartment.

I had been at Serena more than two weeks before I met Manuelo's partner, Dr. Carl Swedenborg. Manuelo had mentioned him, of course, but I had not seen him. One of the reasons was that I had never been in the sanatorium itself, that second floor with its operating rooms and private and semi-private rooms for patients. Manuelo said they did not like visitors wandering about. That I could understand. Women vain enough to undergo plastic surgery would not want to be seen with their blackened eyes and fresh scars unconcealed by dark glasses and bandages. And so, although I had encountered a few nurses and a young intern or two in the elevator or out on the lawns, I had never met Manuelo's partner.

Then, when I entered the apartment one evening, he was there, having a scotch and soda with Manuelo. He got to his feet, a tall man with graying blond hair, thin features, and hazel eyes that held what looked like a settled discontent. Manuelo had said his partner was about his own age, but he looked about ten years older.

Manuelo made the introductions and then

said, "If you'll excuse us for a moment, Sara, we were just finishing up a bit of shoptalk."

"Of course. Don't let me interrupt."

The two men spent several minutes discussing a lipectomy to be performed upon an extremely overweight patient they didn't name. As I sat there silently, I noticed a certain reserve, even a coolness, in their manner toward each other.

At last Dr. Swedenborg put down his empty glass and got to his feet. Manuelo also rose. "Well," Dr. Swedenborg said, "I had best get to bed soon. I want to drive into Milano early tomorrow to look for a car."

"What do you plan to buy?"

"A good used Buick or Olds, if I can find one." There was a certain bitter challenge in the hazel eyes that looked into Manuelo's dark ones. "That's all I can afford."

Manuelo looked coolly back at him. "I hope you find something you like."

Dr. Swedenborg said he was pleased to meet me, and then he left. About fifteen minutes later, as we sat over dinner on the little balcony, I said, "You and Dr. Swedenborg don't like each other very much, do you?"

"Not much."

"Then why do you have him as a partner?"

"Because he's a damned good plastic surgeon. Nobody in the country, including me, is better at rhinoplasty." By then I knew that rhinoplasty meant nose job.

"If he's that good but doesn't like you, why doesn't he go off on his own?"

"Because he'd have a hard time building a practice. Women don't like him. In fact, sometimes after he's performed an operation —one especially suited to his talents—he leaves the operating room before the patient comes out of the anesthetic. The doctor she sees both before and after the operation is me. A deception, yes, but one for the patient's own good. She gets the best surgery possible for her particular case, and yet is spared the knowledge that the surgeon is someone she dislikes."

"*I* didn't like him," I admitted, "although I don't know why." There was nothing really wrong with his appearance or manner, except for the look of chronic fretfulness in his eyes.

"Probably the reason women don't like him is that he doesn't like them."

"You mean he's gay?"

"No. He has a wife and three children

104

about twenty miles down the valley, and he goes home to them at night, unless, like tonight, there is some special reason for him to stay over. Then he uses one of the staff sleeping rooms on the second floor. No, sexually he's hetero, but he doesn't like women as *people*. He doesn't like socializing with them or even being around them any more than necessary, and they sense it immediately."

"I wonder why it is that a man with his temperament chose to be a plastic surgeon."

"I've wondered about it, too. Seems to me he should have specialized in the gall bladder or something."

After a brief knock at the door, Eunice wheeled in the cart bearing dessert and coffee. A waitress on the dinner shift, Eunice stayed an hour late each night to serve dinner to Manuelo and me. She had dark hair and was young and pretty, but then almost the whole domestic staff was attractive, including the pert redhead who served my breakfast each morning. Maria Guerrero, the housekeeper, was about the only exception.

When I had asked Manuelo how his patients liked being surrounded by all this young pulchritude, he said they liked it fine, just as they liked everything in their environment here. "They're not envious, if that's what you're thinking. The women who come here have strong egos. They'd have to have, to lavish as much money on themselves as they do. They figure that they'll leave here looking as good as any of those maids, or almost; *and* they'll still be rich, which probably none of those maids will ever be."

Eunice removed the dinner plates, placed a fluted glass of chocolate mousse before each of us, and set down the coffee pot and two small white cups close to me. Then she wheeled the cart out.

While I was pouring the coffee I thought of what Dr. Swedenborg had said about trying to find a good used car. There had been something accusatory in his "That's all I can afford." Did he feel he did not get his fair share of Serena's profits? I had an impulse to ask Manuelo about it. But sensing that I might hit upon something truly bitter between the two men, something that Manuelo would not want me to know about, I repressed my curiosity. It was not worth the risk of marring in even a small way the lovely hour ahead of us.

Two mornings later I awoke to find the first of the winter rains beating against the window. Plainly, not a day for walking in the hills. After I had eaten the breakfast brought to me by Amy, the redhead whose freckles seemed only to emphasize her prettiness, I set the tray out in the hall. I mended a bra strap, did my nails, and then sat looking at that intricately carved armoire. I did not use it—one of the two large closets was adequate for my needs—but from my first day here I had admired it. Manuelo told me that he had bought it from an antiques dealer when he began furnishing the place, but he could not remember how old it was, or even its country of origin.

Now I went to the wardrobe and opened its doors wide. I had heard that people quite often found in antique furniture—in a drawer or on a shelf—old letters or perhaps a bit of newsprint that gave a clue to the age or origin of the piece. I pulled the dressing-table bench over to the armoire and climbed up on it.

There was something way back there on the shelf, tubular in shape. My fingers touched a roll of stiff paper, which I brought down and spread out on the bed.

A circus poster. I knew that it must be old, not only because the heavy paper was yellowed, but also because of the style of the printing and the absurd costumes—a pair of short, red-and-black striped bloomers worn over red tights—of the man who apparently had been the star of the show.

Across the top of the poster were the words *Gorman Brothers Circus*. Beneath that the bloomered gentleman, apparently having just been expelled from the mouth of a cannon, hurtled, with knees drawn up in a fetal position, across the poster. Beneath him were the words *See Knud Knudsen, the Human Cannonball!*

The rest of the poster was given over to a list of other performers, and it read like a roll call of United Nations delegates: The Gertmanian Brothers, Jugglers Extraordinaire. The Flying Imaris. Juanito el Cuchillo and Constancia. The Demetrios Family. And so on. Across the top of the poster were the words *Coming August 18 to 20*. But it didn't give the year, or the place the circus had been coming to.

I looked at the bloomered man again. Knud Knudsen. A Danish name. What did that remind me of? I had it. Manuelo said that a two-hundred-pound Danish princess had been the last occupant of this room.

What if, when very young, the princess had visited this country? What if she had seen and fallen in love with her fellow Dane, the Human Cannonball? What if, years and many pounds later, she had come back to America, not just to be made beautiful, but to try to find Knud Knudsen?

But why had she left her cherished poster here? Well, suppose she actually had found her Dane. Able to fold him in her ample embrace, what need did she have to this poster?

I found myself smiling at my own fantasy. But come to think of it, the idea of royalty becoming enamored of circus performers was not so farfetched. Queen Caroline, the dotty wife of England's George IV, had actually joined such a traveling show and, as part of its parade, had ridden, bare-breasted, in an open carriage through the streets of Italian cities.

I put the rolled-up poster back on the armoire shelf so that someone else might find and be amused by it when my own occupancy of this room ended.

It would end soon, of course. For a while after Manuelo and I married we might share his apartment. But he had talked a few times of wanting to build a house somewhere on Serena's extensive acreage . . .

Very early in December I took the bus north to Oresburg to spend a few days with my mother in her winter apartment. One day in her Jeep we drove over the rutted road that led to our woodland house. There it sat, roof weighted with snow, in an ermine-white clearing unmarked by anything except the tracks of rabbits and deer and other wild creatures.

As my mother looked wistfully at the little house, I knew she must be remembering a time lost to my conscious memory, a time when my young father had been alive and there had been no winter apartment in town, no weekend job at the Silver Nugget, just herself and her small daughter and her beloved husband in this woodland house.

Behind us in the rear seat Charlie—muzzle gray and legs stiff now—gave a bark, as if he too were remembering the days when he had raced about this clearing or lain beside the fire in that old house. Mother started the jeep's engine, and we drove back to town.

During my stay with her, she didn't once ask if I had been going to bed with Manuelo. She must have known the answer. It must have been plain in my eyes and voice when I spoke his name—and, as is the way with people in love, I spoke his name at every opportunity.

My last night there, Mother said, "You'll be home for Christmas, won't you? Dr.— Dr. Covarrubias would be welcome, too."

"Manuelo, Mother! He'll want you to call him that. And listen, Mother. He wants you to come to Serena for Christmas."

She looked bewildered. "To the sanatorium?"

"Yes! Manuelo says Christmas is wonderful there. On Christmas Eve there's a special dinner for the patients, the ones who are up and about, I mean. On Christmas Day there's open house on the whole lower floor. It's for the staff and their relatives, and anybody from the neighboring ranches who wants to come, and tradesmen from Milano, that little town I told you about."

"But a party like that, in a sanatorium! What about the patients who are recovering from operations?"

"The whole second floor is sound-proofed."

"But what about all those rich women who aren't in bed, the ones who listen to you play? Do they like a party where almost anybody—"

"The ones who don't can always drive off someplace for a few hours, or retire to the third floor. But most of them, Manuelo says,

111

seem to enjoy the open house. He thinks that some of them feel it's an upper-class sort of thing to do—you know, the gentry going to the servants' hall to help them celebrate Christmas. Please, Mother! Please say you'll come."

After a while she said, "All right. I guess it's all to the good for me to see what— Yes, I'll come."

9

On Christmas Eve in the big dining room, fragrant with pine wreaths hung on the paneled walls, I played Christmas carols for the formally gowned patients, and for my mother. Especially for her I played—sandwiched in between "Silent Night" and "White Christmas"—Rachmaninoff's Second Concerto, which had been her favorite ever since I played my first halting rendition of it at the age of twelve.

You might have thought she would seem out of place among these brittle rich women. After all, she wore the only long dress she owned, a dark blue velvet one showing its eight years of wear. She looked her actual age, forty-two, here among these women who, at least from several feet away, looked about twenty-five. But that same natural dignity that kept the drunks at the Silver Nugget at bay served her here, too.

While the dessert, a flaming cherries jubilee, was being served, Manuelo did something I had never seen him do before. He came into the dining room and sat down at a table, the table where my mother had been placed with two other women. It was close enough to the piano that, between numbers, I could hear the conversation. He was giving most of his attention to my mother. I soon realized that he was not treating her in the overly deferential manner another man might have showed the mother of his lover. Instead he was treating her as a contemporary—which indeed she was—and as someone interesting and attractive in her own right. The grateful love I felt for him made my throat tighten up.

The next day was noisy, rowdy, and great fun. A four-piece band played country-western music—music as raw and strong as a shot of straight whiskey—for dancing in the broad entrance hall. Staff members, including kitchen staff I had never seen before, were there. So were their brothers and their sisters and their cousins and their aunts. A few people from cattle ranches in the area attended, and so did at least a dozen Milano tradesmen.

But the big surprise was Patrick Murray. I wanted to think that our conversations out in the hills had lessened his sense of grievance. Anyway, he showed up—in kilts, no less, and carrying an Irish bagpipe. Asked to play, he readily assented, but first told a little story. The Irish, he said, had invented the pipes as a joke, and later presented them to the Scots. But the Scotsmen had never caught on to the joke, and so made the bagpipes their national instrument. He played after that, and one of the busboys and Amy, the freckle-faced redhead who brought me my breakfast each morning, did an Irish jig. Later, out in the hall, Patrick danced with several people, including my mother and me, to the band's rendition of tunes like "Tie a Yellow Ribbon."

Among the past and present patients of Manuelo's who joined the festivities was Elisa Dalton, accompanied by a man I heard someone identify as Keith Chardine, her absurdly jealous young husband. A short but well-built young man with curly dark hair that brushed his collar in back, he appeared to be somewhat younger than thirty. Once,

114

when his wife was dancing with Manuelo, I saw him leaning against the wall, arms crossed, dark fury in his eyes. I felt sorry for him. His wife, her lashes half veiling her eyes as she smiled up at Manuelo, obviously was angling for an amorous response from her partner and a furious one from her husband. I was pleased to see that she was only halfway successful. Manuelo's manner was courteous but ever so faintly touched with boredom.

Late that afternoon I drove my mother up to the highway to catch the bus to Oresburg. As we waited in the fading light, she said, "Sara, I have to ask you this. Are you and Manuelo going to be married?"

"Yes, I'm almost certain so. It's as I told you. He's been divorced twice. He wants to be sure this time. And I want him to be."

"Oh, Sara. Please, try to—I want you safe, darling. I want it far more than I wanted—"

She broke off. During my last visit to Oresburg, and her two days at Serena, she had not once mentioned her disappointed hopes about my music. Plainly, she didn't want to bring the subject up at this last moment.

For a few seconds she was silent, her blue eyes looking up into mine. Then she said,

"Oh, there it is." We kissed and embraced. Then I put her aboard the bus.

10

That Christmas had been so enchanting. It seemed ironic indeed that within days my wonderful world started to collapse.

At first I had cause only for a faint unease. Twice in one week Amy delivered notes from Manuelo along with my breakfast. Both said that he would be working late. It would be best, he had written, for me to have dinner in my room. He himself would dine on the second floor with the staff.

I accepted that. Earlier he had told me that there was often a rush of new patients after the holidays. Women who had planned to spend their spouses' five-figure Christmas checks on Alaskan fox or diamond-studded watches decided instead to have their breasts lifted or their eyelids smoothed out before going to Palm Springs or Jamaica or the south of France for the rest of the winter.

The next week Manuelo and I had dinner together only once. And when that meal was over he said he was very, very tired. Would I mind if he just went to bed?

The morning after that there was another note, pleading the press of work. But before my dinner arrived in my room I looked out the side window and saw Manuelo's BMW emerging from the sanatorium's sprawling garage. From the front window I watched the car move down the drive to the pillared entrance and the dirt road beyond.

Impossible now to ignore the cold fear spreading inside me, a fear that took all pleasure out of my walks over hills now greening from January rains, and all life out of my piano playing, so that my hearers began to give me strange looks. Or perhaps it was not my playing. Perhaps it was something stricken in my face that brought those looks to theirs—in some cases speculative, in some pitying, in others ironically amused.

The last few days in January Manuelo came down with a bad case of flu. Half ashamed of myself, I realized that I was glad of his illness. With all the sanatorium staff already overworked, he seemed grateful for my services. Except when I was at the piano, I spent all my waking hours with him. I read aloud to him from books on his living room shelves, and from whatever magazines were in the daily mail. (Mrs. Guerrero, her face holding a concern that reminded me their association dated back forty years, personally brought the mail to his apartment each morning.) Seated at his bedside, I had my meals at the same time he did. I brought him hot and cold liquids, and, when he complained of an ache between his shoulders, massaged the broad tan back with its muscles rippling beneath silky smooth skin.

Once he dispatched me down to the second floor for some sort of new medicine he wanted to try. For the first time I saw the strictly medical part of the sanatorium, with its wide gleaming corridors, and its bandage-swathed patients looking like battlefield casualties as they sat in wheelchairs or lay behind half-closed doors in flower filled rooms.

Still another time, obviously disturbed by something he had read in his newly arrived copy of *Business Week*, he asked me to bring him a blue envelope from his safe. "You'll find it behind that hunting print to the right of the fireplace."

He gave me the combination, a series of numbers I remembered long enough to go to the safe and open it. The blue envelope was on top of a pile of manila ones. I took it out and was about to close the door when something arrested my attention. One end of a business-size envelope protruded a fraction of an inch from beneath the green felt that lined the floor of the safe. Almost automatically, I drew it out.

Manuelo had written on the envelope in his firm, bold hand: "To be sent to the General of the U.S. Army Medical Corps in the event of my death."

I stared at it, feeling a chill spread through me. People usually did not prepare such communications unless they felt themselves to be under some sort of threat—

"Sara!" His voice was weak and hoarse. "Couldn't you get the safe open?"

"Yes. I'm coming right now."

I thrust the white envelope back under the felt lining. I took the big blue envelope and, leaving the safe door open, went into the bedroom. Manuelo took some printed documents, evidently stock certificates, from the envelope and frowned over them for a few minutes. At last, thrusting the certificates back into the envelope, he said, "I think I'll leave things be for now." He handed the envelope back to me.

Back in the living room, I hesitated a moment before the open safe. Anything that concerned Manuelo concerned me. If he was in danger, I had a right to know about it. I replaced the envelope of stock certificates. Then, again leaving the safe open, I returned to his bedside.

About a half hour later he fell asleep. I went out into the living room and slipped the white envelope from beneath the felt. To my surprise I found that it was unsealed. Perhaps Manuelo had thought he might want to add later to its contents. I withdrew the single sheet of typewritten paper. At the top were the printed words *Serena Sanatorium*, and in the right-hand corner a typewritten date of a little more than five years ago.

To whom it may concern:

On April 9, 1975, I was operating on battle casualties at a field hospital fifteen miles from Hue, Vietnam. Among the several other Medical Corpsmen present was Dr. Carl Swedenborg, First Lieutenant.

Enemy mortar fire began. Shells landed at one end of the hospital. Dr. Swedenborg suddenly dropped his instruments and ran from the hospital, leaving his patient, a man with a severe stomach wound, stretched unconscious on the table.

An hour later Dr. Swedenborg was

found cowering in the jungle. By that time his patient had died.

Among other Medical Corps personnel who witnessed this incident were—

Several names followed, those of two or three sergeants and a corporal, if I remember correctly.

Manuelo had signed the document Manuelo D. Covarrubias, M. D., formerly Captain, U.S. Army Medical Corps.

With cold and growing dismay, I read the statement through again. What would happen to Dr. Swedenborg if this document ever reached official hands? Could he still be court-martialed, all these years later? I thought not. But almost certainly he would lose his license to practice medicine.

Why hadn't Manuelo reported at the time his fellow officer's dereliction of duty? And, not having reported it, why was he keeping this unsent statement now? Did Carl Swedenborg know of its existence? Was that how Manuelo managed to keep the services—perhaps underpaid services—of a man who had surgical skill but no bedside manner?

But that was—

I couldn't say the word, even to myself.

And I dared not ask Manuelo about the

document. If I did so, surely that frightening chasm between us would grow even wider. I slipped the envelope back beneath the green felt, closed the safe, and went into the bedroom to sit beside my sleeping lover. Someday he would explain the whole matter to me.

That night, after Eunice had removed our dinner trays, Manuelo's slightly feverish hand grasped mine. "You're not only lovely and charming, Sara. You're a *good* person. There aren't many people, I think, who can be called that."

I walked to my room a few minutes later, feeling that my feet scarcely touched the carpet. Feeling glad, too, that I had not jeopardized my happiness by asking him about something which, I was sure, he would regard as none of my business.

When I came to his apartment two mornings later, I found him up and dressed. "I was hungry as a wolf, so I called down an hour ago and had my breakfast sent up. Yours will be brought to your room. Okay?"

Disconcerted, I said mechanically, "Of course. But should you be up and—"

"Now, Sara! You're not the doctor. I am. I feel a little shaky, but otherwise all right."

That was the way he looked—thinner than

before the flu, and a little pale under his perpetual tan, but otherwise quite recovered.

"I'd best take it slow my first day back at the salt mine, and get to bed early." His smile was warm and easy, but his dark eyes had distanced themselves from me. "That okay?"

"Yes," I said, still in that mechanical voice, and then added, "Don't work too hard."

That miserable day seemed endless. I walked over the hills, blind to the beauty of long green grass and the first of the spring wildflowers. I encountered Patrick Murray and tried to force a smile when he told me, for the third time, the story about the Irishman who lay in wait to shoot his landlord. I played pop songs for the ladies during cocktails and Strauss waltzes at dinner, not feeling the music in the least, finding the notes only through long practice. And that night in my room I could not eat my solitary meal.

Manuelo and I did have dinner together the next night, but during the course of it he mentioned, first, that he again should get to sleep early, and, second, that the next two afternoons he would attend a medical symposium in San Jose. Both days he would not return to Serena until close to midnight.

Thus it was that I did not see him at all again until I saw him with the girl.

11

More for distraction than anything else, I had driven into Milano that morning. After some listless window shopping, I went into the Peppermill, one of the newly opened lunch-and-dinner spots.

It was busy. A waiter showed me to one of the few vacant chairs, at a table for two against the wall. He gave me a menu and left. Before reading it, I looked around.

Manuelo and a girl sat at a table near the center of the room.

From that angle I could see the girl almost full-face. And, oh, she was lovely! Dark hair waving back from a classically perfect face. Great gray eyes beneath winged black brows. But it was not just beauty that made her face so arresting. It was a certain tragic quality. Strange to think of anyone that young—she was my age at most, probably less—as tragic-looking. But the mark of some dark and painful memory was there, both in her eyes and her vulnerable-looking mouth. It was there even when she smiled.

I loathed her, of course. I wished she had never been born. And yet even I could not help but be touched by that hurt, fragile quality of hers.

And there was something else about her. I had seen her before. Where, I couldn't say. Perhaps it had been on a TV or movie screen, but I had seen her.

Manuelo's entire profile was not visible to me, but I could see enough of it to tell how ardently he looked at that gray-eyed girl. Time was, back before I'd left the music academy for Serena, when he had looked at me like that.

Something, perhaps the intensity of my gaze, made him turn that handsome face toward me. I saw dismay leap into his dark eyes, and then anger, and then a cold hardness.

I dropped the menu on the table and almost ran from the restaurant.

By seven-fifty that night the last of the patients had left the dining room. I went upstairs. As I had expected, there was a knock at my door a few minutes later.

"Come in."

Manuelo walked into the room. Seated at

125

my dressing table with a comb in my hand, I did not get up.

"About today," he said.

I had sworn I would not be the first to mention that girl.

He waited, but I remained stubbornly silent. After a few seconds he said, "I was with Gabriella Montgomery. She's the daughter of some old friends of mine who live in San Jose."

"Oh, yes. Where you said you were going to be attending a medical convention." I had wanted to speak dryly. Instead the words came out thick with pain and rage.

He shrugged and then said, "Sara, people can't help falling in love."

"Until a short time ago, I thought you loved me."

"And I did! But love doesn't always last."

"Apparently not, but I thought it would last more than two or three months." It gave me almost physical pain to speak the words. "Especially since I was under the impression that you planned to marry me."

"Sara, did I ever promise to marry you?"

"No."

"Did I ever actually promise you anything, except a rather handsome stipend for playing the piano in attractive surround-ings?"

"No. What, by the way, have you prom-ised this Gabriella?"

"Nothing, as yet."

"Oh, yes. I remember your being rather frank about your technique. If you figure they're worth only a one-night stand, you give them the big rush. But with the others you hold off, until they're practically beg-ging you to take them to bed."

Genuine surprise showed in his face. "You sound—almost hard. I've always thought of you as so young and soft—"

"You give a good course in growing up fast, mister. What do you want me to do? Leave first thing in the morning?"

"Of course not."

"I thought you might want my room for Gabriella."

"Oh, no. She wouldn't be staying—" He broke off and then said, "There's no reason you should quit your job. My ladies like you, and surely you must like the pay and the surroundings."

As I opened my mouth to speak, he went on, "Don't answer now. Think it over. We'll talk tomorrow."

He left the room. I began to pace the floor.

For a while I was fiercely glad that I had not wept, that instead I had managed to strike him as cynical, even hard. Then reaction set in. I was not cynical, not hard. All I wanted in the whole world was to be in his arms. Maybe if I had showed that, maybe if I had wept, I could have made him feel that he had not only loved me but still loved me.

In the end, of course, I sped down the hall and started to knock on his door. Then I halted, fist poised.

There was someone with him, and both he and his visitor were very angry. In Manuelo's case it was a controlled anger, his voice pitched low enough that although I could hear the steely tone, I could not distinguish the words. The other voice, shaking with fury, was pitched even lower, so low that I could not be sure whether it belonged to a man or a rage-choked woman.

By intruding now I would scarcely endear myself to him. In fact, it suddenly seemed to me absurd that I had thought of going to him tonight, whether or not he was alone. The only result would have been the loss of whatever remained of my dignity.

Minutes after I returned to my room, there was another knock on the door. I opened it, sure that it was Eunice with my dinner tray. It was. She gave me a swift look and then lowered her gaze to the tray. Plainly she knew that Manuelo and I were no longer lovers. Probably by now the whole sanatorium knew it.

I threw a swift look down the long hall, wondering if Manuelo's visitor was still there. I wondered, too, if Eunice had served dinner to the two of them or to Manuelo alone. Probably neither was the case. Probably, he had gone off earlier to have dinner someplace with Gabriella.

I took the tray, thanked Eunice, and closed the door. The Beef Stroganoff she had brought, along with green beans, seemed to have no taste whatsoever. After a few mouthfuls I put the tray outside my door. Then, because I could think of nothing else to do, I went to bed.

But not to sleep, of course. I stared numbly at the invisible ceiling, unable to plan what to do with the rest of my life, unable even to visualize a life without Manuelo and the hope of being with him always.

Finally, as gray dawn light filled the room, I fell asleep, but only for about two hours. When I awoke to ironically bright sunlight

I saw a note under my door. I got out of bed and unfolded it.

It was from him:

Dear Sara,

Will you please join me for dinner in my apartment at eight tonight? We should discuss your plans for the future.

Manuelo

So that was how he wanted to end it, business-like but amiably. Perhaps he would offer me an increase in salary, or a "loan" to help me resume my studies at the music academy.

I passed the rest of the morning like a sleepwalker. All I really recall of it is sitting alone on that bench built around the live oak up on the hillside. Manuelo's BMW drove around the corner of the sanatorium. He stopped, got out, and spoke for a minute or so with a couple of patients seated in lawn chairs. Then he drove out the gate along the narrow road toward the highway.

Around one, with that same sense of sleepwalking, I returned to my room. A tray on the bedside table held a ham sandwich and a glass of milk. I felt dull gratitude. Evidently when she brought my breakfast tray

—which I had barely touched—Amy realized from the look of me that I would not want to join all those chattering, covertly curious women at the buffet lunch downstairs.

To my faint surprise, I found that I could eat all of the sandwich and drink the milk. I placed the tray out in the hall and fell across my bed. The effects of my long wakefulness the night before struck me, and I went almost instantly to sleep.

When I awoke it was four-twenty. Despite a dull headache, I took a shower and then changed into the pink outfit I had worn for my first day's work here. Somehow I managed to play for both cocktails and dinner, although all I clearly remember of those hours is seeing Elisa Dalton and her sullenly handsome young husband seated at one of the dinner tables. I felt a stab of envy, not of Elisa's fame or money, but of the fact that she had a man so devoted to her that he would accompany her to Serena, despite the jealous torments such visits must bring him.

When the last diners left their table, I rode up in the elevator. In my own room I waited for a few minutes until my watch hands pointed exactly to eight o'clock, the time specified in Manuelo's note. Then I walked down the empty hallway and knocked on his apartment door.

No answer. I knocked again. Still no answer. I opened the door and entered the big living room, illuminated tonight only by a heavily shaded lamp on the refectory table. No glitter of candles out on the balcony where, with dinner, we had begun evenings so lovely that their memory made my heart twist. Perhaps he had deemed it an inappropriate setting for what he had to say, and so had planned to tell Eunice, when she came in, to put placemats on the refectory table. Nevertheless, I started toward the balcony.

In that dim light I was within a few feet of Manuelo before I saw him. He was stretched out on his stomach, arms crooked at the elbows, the left side of his face resting against the Kerman rug.

Something protruded from his sports coat, between the shoulder blades.

I don't know what told me he was dead. Something in the attitude of his body? Some sixth sense of my own?

And I don't remember screaming. But I must have screamed again and again, because after an unmeasured interval I became aware that my throat felt raw, and the room had filled with people. A young man I recognized as an intern knelt beside Manuelo, his fingers on the brown muscular wrist. "No pulse," he said to a man who stood near him.

"Don't touch anything else!" the man answered, and I realized he was Carl Swedenborg. He no longer had his faintly fretful air. Instead his face was pale and stern. "Don't touch anything. Above all, don't remove that knife."

Knife? Oh, yes, the knife whose handle protruded—

I heard Dr. Swedenborg ask if anyone had called the police. Someone—I don't know who—said yes. Then someone—again I didn't know who—was leading me through the crowd to the door. I saw Mrs. Guerrero, looking so white that I realized that for her it must be almost as if her son lay there on the floor. I saw Eunice, who about now should have been serving dinner to Manuelo and me. I saw Amy, her face so pale that her freckles seemed to stand out. Then I was being led down the hall to my room. Looking down, I saw that the person who grasped my arm wore white stockings and shoes. I realized then that she must be a nurse.

We went into my room. She said, "Are you all right?"

I nodded.

"Sure you don't feel faint?" She was a middle-aged woman with dyed red hair and a kind face.

Again I nodded.

"Then probably the best thing for you to do is to just sit here quietly for a while."

She went out, closing the door behind her.

12

A sense of timelessness settled over me as I sat there in the glare of my room's overhead light. (Who had turned it on, I or the nurse? The nurse, probably.) Sirens were approaching now, only to fall silent as they neared the entrance to the sanatorium grounds. People moved up and down the hallway outside my room. Now and then I heard voices. Now and then I heard a door close.

Once, the door-closing sound—a metallic sound—came from somewhere outside. I got to my feet and looked out the window above the empty fishpond. A white ambulance had appeared from around the building's rear corner and was moving along the side drive toward the semicircular one in front. They were taking Manuelo away. Manuelo, whose handsome face and smoothly muscled body had seemed so alive that one might have thought he would never die.

I sank back into my chair. I don't know what time it was when someone knocked. I said, "Come in."

He did. "Hello, Miss Hargreaves. That's right, isn't it, Sara Hargreaves?"

"Yes."

"I'm County Detective Arthur Denken." He took a sort of leather wallet from an inside coat pocket and flipped it open. I saw the metallic glitter of a badge. He restored it to his pocket.

He didn't look like my idea of a policeman. He was a thin, dark man of about forty-five, dressed in a well-worn but fairly expensive looking charcoal gray suit. "May I sit down?" he asked.

I nodded. Sitting down on the dressing table bench, he took from another pocket a small notebook covered in worn black leather. Clipped to it was a ballpoint pen.

"Now, as I understand it, you were the one who found the—who found Dr. Covarrubias."

I nodded.

"Why had you gone to his apartment?"

"He left a note under my door this morning. I think it's there on the dressing table."

He picked up the note, read it swiftly, laid it down, and then wrote something in his notebook. "He was alone when you found him?"

I nodded.

"They tell me you play the piano for the guests—I suppose I should call them patients —here at the sanatorium."

"Yes."

"But I gather you were more than Dr. Covarrubias's employee. You and he were—"

"Yes," I said dully, "we were."

"What did his note mean about discussing plans for your future?"

"I guess he meant—whether or not I should stay on here."

"Why shouldn't you have stayed on?"

I would have to explain about that, sooner or later. Besides, he must already know the answer. Plenty of people would have been able to tell him.

"He'd fallen out of love with me. In fact, he said he—he loved someone else."

"I see."

His face was expressionless. "Who could have done that to him!" I cried. "Who could have hated him enough to—to—"

136

"That's what we intend to find out, Miss Hargreaves. Now we are taking as many fingerprints as we can tonight. The rest will be done tomorrow. No one is to leave the premises until the job is finished." He paused. "Is it all right if I send someone right now to get your prints?"

"Yes."

He stood up. "Have you had any dinner?"

I thought for a moment. "No."

"Want me to see to it that some food is sent up to you?"

"Thank you. I couldn't eat."

"All right. Oh, one thing more. I'd rather you didn't leave your room tomorrow until you and I have had another talk. I'll see to it that someone brings your meals."

I nodded.

"Very well, then. Good night, Miss Hargreaves." He left.

After a while someone came to take my fingerprints. To my surprise, it was a woman, a middle-aged brunette with a reserved, even prim, manner. She spoke as little as possible while she pressed my fingertips one by one onto an inked pad, then onto a strip of paper. She gave me a tissue to wipe the ink away.

When she had gone I undressed, went to

bed, and lay awake staring into the darkness. A merciful sense of unreality still held me, but I knew that pain was out there somewhere, waiting to pounce. And I knew that in much the same way, outside the walls of this now-quiet building, patrolling men waited to pounce upon anyone who might try to slip away . . .

Some time toward morning fatigue overcame me and I slept. A knock awakened me to flooding sunlight. For a moment, not remembering what had happened, I just thought it was Amy, with my breakfast.

"Come in."

She moved quietly into the room. Not looking at me, she placed my tray on the bedside table. For just a moment her gaze slid toward me, and I realized with incredulity that she appeared to be afraid. Struck dumb, I didn't even thank her as she hurried from the room. Afraid! Why should she or anyone appear to be afraid of me?

A little more than eight hours later I learned the answer to that question.

The short winter day was fading when Detective Denken and a uniformed policewoman came into that pretty room. He told me that I was under arrest for the murder of Manuelo Covarrubias. He said that I had the right to remain silent, and the right to legal counsel. Feeling as if we were three figures in a dream, I thought—oh, yes. They call that the Miranda rights.

I said, "There's been a mistake."

"I'm afraid not, Miss Hargreaves. Your fingerprints and no one else's are all over the handle of that knife."

"Knife?"

"The knife from that case of ivory-handled knives. The knife you used to kill Dr. Covarrubias."

I said, with a kind of weird calm, "I never even touched any of those knives. Not once. Ever."

"We're taking you out the back way, Miss Hargreaves. No need to parade you through the whole place. And if you'll promise not to make any trouble, we'll leave off the handcuffs."

13

My mother came to see me in the jail at Riverview, the county seat, the next morning. I don't think it was until I entered the room where she waited, trying to smile, that I fully realized what had happened to me.

Terror descended upon me then, but it was terror more for her than for myself. Her white face looked ten years older than it had when I had put her on the bus that previous Christmas.

Crying, we held each other for perhaps two minutes. Then we sat facing each other at one corner of a varnished table, both of her hands clasping mine. Trying to ignore the barred windows and the uniformed policeman standing with back turned to us outside the barred door, I said, "Mother, I didn't—I didn't—"

"Oh, my baby! Do you think I ever believed for one moment that you did do it? If only I could get you out of this awful place! But they've set bail at—"

"I know. A hundred fifty thousand. But this place isn't so bad. Honestly it isn't."

That was the case. True, at the other end of the row of cells two women had quarreled most of the night. But there had been few of the things I had feared as, seated in the back seat with the policewoman, I rode away from the sanatorium. I saw no rats, or even cockroaches. My cellmate was neither noisy nor abusive. Instead she was a middle-aged woman who told me she was charged with forgery and then said, "But I'd rather not

140

talk about it. In fact, I'd rather not talk, period." Then she had returned to the paperback she was reading.

Now my mother said, "Sara, I'm going to hire a lawyer."

"The court has appointed one. He's coming here later this—"

"I'm not going to have you defended by some court-appointed lawyer!"

"But, Mother! We can't afford—"

"We can! He's Mr. Burford's nephew." Mr. Burford, who long ago had been promoted from assistant manager to manager of the Oresburg mine, had been my mother's employer for almost half her life. "Mr. Burford says he's one of the best defense lawyers in the state."

"But how can we pay—"

"Mr. Burford will loan us the money. I can pay it back a little at a time from my salary."

And how many years will that take, I thought.

She must have read my mind, because she said, "Don't you see, darling? If anything —bad happened to you, money wouldn't matter. Nothing would matter."

The next day in that same room I conferred with Mr. Burford's nephew. His name was Leonard Coombs. He was very thin, and his dirty blond hair kept standing up in a cowlick, no matter how often he smoothed it down with his long, big-knuckled hand. His blue-gray eyes had a trick of staring at you fixedly through tortoise-rimmed glasses. My mother had told me he was in his mid-forties, but there was something awkward and appealing about him that gave him the air of an earnest schoolboy. Maybe that was what made juries trust him.

But right from the start he made it clear that he had almost no hope of getting me off scot-free. "Not unless you can give me some innocent explanation of why your prints were all over the handle of that knife."

"I can't." I smoothed my hand over a pleat in my green woolen skirt. It had been in the package of garments Mrs. Guerrero had sent from Serena, so that I could have changes of clothing while I awaited trial. "I just know I never touched that knife, or any of the knives in that case."

"My dear girl, you must have. There is no way, no way at all, that anyone could have faked your fingerprints. Of course—" He broke off.

"Yes?"

"Have you ever heard of a fugue?"

"Of course. It's a polyphonic composition developed from a given theme, according to strict—"

"No, no! I don't mean fugue as a musical term. I'm speaking of it in the psychiatric sense. It's an interval when a person, in a trance state, may perform acts lost to conscious memory."

I considered. Could it be that sometime —perhaps during the days when Manuelo had the flu—I had gone to that case, and opened it, and handled that knife—

"No!" I cried. "That couldn't have happened. I've always hated knives, guns, swords, things like that."

Leonard Coombs sighed. "All right. Anyway, the fugue theory wouldn't help us much. It might explain how you had innocently put your fingerprints on that knife handle. But it wouldn't explain why they were still there—your unblurred prints and no one else's—when he was found stabbed to death.

"Of course," he went on, "you could always plead not guilty by reason of temporary insanity. His treatment of you had driven you over the brink and so you grabbed the knife and—"

"No! *Nothing* like that happened. I walked

143

into his apartment and found him lying there, that's all." At the memory, everything inside me seemed to tighten up.

"All right. We'll come back to that later. Now can you think of anyone elsg who might have done it?"

Anyone else. Anyone besides myself, he meant, who might have had both motive and opportunity. Because I certainly had had them both. And far more damning than the other two, there were those fingerprints. I had a sense of being hemmed in, as if the walls of this ugly room, with its dirty barred windows and cigarette-scarred furniture, were drawing closer together.

To ward off that feeling, I said quickly, "There were people who had a grudge against Manuelo." When he looked at me expectantly, I went on, "There's Patrick Murray. He once owned the land the sanatorium is on. He feels Manuelo didn't pay a fair price for it."

"How long ago did Covarrubias buy it?"

"I don't know. The sanatorium was built about ten years ago, I think."

He shook his head. "If this Murray was going to take revenge, it seems unlikely he would have waited that long. Anyone else?"

A memory of my first evening at Serena

144

flashed through my mind. I told Leonard Coombs about Paula Winship—the ruined upper half of her face, her masking black glasses, her bitterness.

"You said Winship? The wife of the airplane manufacturer?"

I nodded.

"It should be easy enough to check whether or not she could have been anywhere near the sanatorium that night. Who else?"

I told him about Keith Chardine, Elisa Dalton's almost pathologically jealous young husband. "And they *were* there that night. At least they had been earlier that evening."

"I'll check on them, too. Anyone else?"

"Manuelo's partner."

The interest in the blue-gray eyes behind the glasses sharpened. "His partner!"

I told him about finding that document in Manuelo's safe.

Leonard Coombs said, "That apartment must have been searched thoroughly. Probably the District Attorney's office has that document now. I'll find out. Certainly it gives Carl Swedenborg a strong motive. If Covarrubias had been using that Vietnam incident to exploit him all these years—"

He broke off, and then added, "Of course,

145

it wouldn't explain your fingerprints, would it?" He rose, picked up his briefcase. "But anyway, I'll ask the D.A. about that statement."

Two mornings later we conferred in that same room. "First I'll give you the good news. Your bail has been posted. You're getting out of here."

Amazed relief washed over me. Even though it was not as bad as I had feared, jail still was not a pleasant place. Noise was almost continuous. Shouts, laughter, fights, radios. The food was not actually inedible, but almost. And that morning my cellmate had broken her silence long enough to say that her trial was coming up the next week, and that she expected to be tried and sentenced all in one day. Who, I had wondered, would be sharing my cell after that?

Now I said, "My bail's been posted! But how on earth—" Who did I know who would risk a hundred fifty thousand on my behalf?

"Mr. Patrick Murray posted it."

I felt an incredulous gratitude. Had he really come to like me that much during our walks through the low hills? Then, remembering the bitterness he had expressed toward Manuelo, I wondered if he thought me

146

guilty—and therefore worthy of his generosity.

"I've arranged for you to live in a small apartment near the courthouse until your trial is over." He paused. "Now for the bad news. Paula Winship was on her way to a big charity ball in Santa Barbara at the time Covarrubias was killed. As for Elisa Dalton and Keith Chardine, they say they left the Serena dining room early, before they'd had dessert, and drove straight to a friend's house nearby, arriving almost exactly at eight. The friend confirms that. Of course, they still *could* have had enough time for one or both of them to sneak up to Covarrubias's apartment and stab him, but it seems unlikely."

I gave a vague nod! That night I had been far too miserable to know who had left the dining room when.

"As for the document about Dr. Swedenborg that you described to me, the D.A.'s office says that no such document was found in Covarrubias' safe or anywhere else in his apartment."

"But it was there, right where I told you, under the felt on the bottom of the safe! Maybe I was careless in putting it back. I mean, Manuelo might have seen later that it had been moved, and so decided to put it in a safe deposit box. Maybe he destroyed it. Or maybe Dr. Swedenborg—"

"I know. Maybe he managed to get hold of the document before the apartment was searched. But in any case, all we have now is your unsupported statement that there even was such a document. Of course, if you could remember the names of those other Medical Corps members, the ones Covarrubias listed as having seen Swedenborg desert his patient under fire—"

"I've tried and tried, but I can't."

"Well, even if you could, it probably wouldn't do us any good. I don't think the Army would want to try to trace them for us, just because you say they may have witnessed a certain incident clear back in the seventies. If you had *anything* to back your story up—But you haven't."

"No," I said dully.

"And so if we brought your story about Swedenborg up at the trial, it would actually work against us. It would look as if you were so desperate that, with no evidence to back you, you were trying to shift the blame to a respected doctor, with no concern about what you might be doing to his reputation and career."

After a moment Leonard Coombs added, "Have you been able to think of anyone else who might be guilty?"

I said, with an effort, "No. But Manuelo was very attractive. He must have aroused jealousy in a lot of men. I mean, there were so many women in his life—"

"Including Gabriella Montgomery."

My head jerked up in surprise. As nearly as I could remember, I had not mentioned her to him, not by name.

"I've been talking to people at the sanatorium, remember. It seems that almost everyone there knew that Covarrubias was pursuing a San Jose girl named Gabriella Montgomery."

"Are you thinking about—"

"Putting her on the stand? Lord, no. I've checked her out. Socially prominent family. Just turned eighteen. Went to convent school. Probably a virgin. Like Dr. Swedenborg, she'd do you more harm than good. The jury would resent a young girl like her being brought into the case."

After a moment he added hopefully, "Have you changed your mind? Will you let me plead you not guilty by reason of temporary insanity? It's the only way I'll have a chance of getting you off completely."

I shook my head. "I didn't do it. Sane or insane, I just didn't do it."

He sighed. "All right. I'll play to the jury's sympathies as much as possible, in the hopes they'll go easy on you."

14

And at my trial a little more than a month later, that was exactly what he did.

Whenever I think of that trial, the first thing I recall is the heat. A spell of unseasonable April warmth had descended upon the San Joaquin Valley. Either the country courthouse was not air conditioned or the system had gone on the blink. At any rate, the room was sweltering.

The second thing I recall is the sense of row upon row of people behind me, avid people, silent, drawn by a trial that, as the TV commentators put it, had everything—attractive young defendant; handsome, philandering victim; and, as a background, a sanatorium filled with women who were rich or fashionable or famous or all three. I almost never turned around from the defense table except to smile once in a while at my white-faced mother, but I never lost my sense of those silent spectators.

I knew that Patrick Murray was not among them. I had written a grateful letter to him, suggesting that he come to see me. He had replied that he was going to a hot springs resort in Georgia for several months in the hope of ridding himself of the rheumatism that had plagued him for years. He thanked me and wished me luck at my trial.

Day after sweltering day in that courtroom, Leonard Coombs did his best for me. He put me on the stand to describe how, the night before Manuelo's death, I had heard quarreling voices in his apartment. I described, too, how the next night I had entered that big, dimly lighted room and seen him lying on the floor.

Any one of scores of people could have been in that apartment a few minutes before me, Leonard pointed out. It didn't have to be a patient or a member of the medical or domestic staffs. The sanatorium's entrance doors were not locked until eleven at night, and so up until then almost anyone could have gotten inside the building.

As for the fingerprints, Leonard confined himself to vague hints that under certain circumstances fingerprints could be forged—a suggestion that brought a tolerant smile to the District Attorney's face. Except for those hints, Leonard limited himself to appeals to the jury's compassion. Here was a talented young girl, he said, who'd had the misfortune to meet a practiced seducer more than twice her age. He had appeared to promise her both enduring love and marriage, and then, with callous abruptness, had told her he was through with her. Leonard's tactics seemed to be working, at least with the women jurors. I saw unmistakable sympathy in the eyes of at least two of them.

The District Attorney, as if sure of getting some kind of conviction, called only a few witnesses. The first was the medical examiner, who testified that Manuelo had died between seven and seven-fifty that February night. After him came the fingerprint experts, who said that my fingerprints—and my fingerprints only—had been found on the knife handle. Next came Eunice, who testified about those dinners on the glassed-in balcony. She also stated that she was the one who had found me screaming as I looked down at Manuelo lying on the Oriental rug.

The next witness was Detective Denken, who testified that in the course of his first interview with me I had showed him Manuelo's note asking me to come to his place at eight that night.

"You say she had saved it, placed it on her dressing table? Perhaps as if she'd been prepared to prove that she had reason for going to the deceased's apartment?"

"Objection," Leonard Coombs said quickly. "Calls for a conclusion by the witness."

"Sustained."

To my surprise, the fifth witness called by the District Attorney, apparently to underline the fact that I had ample motivation, was Elisa Dalton. She testified that "all the patients" at Serena had been talking about how Dr. Covarrubias had found "a new young girl" and was throwing Sara Hargreaves over. The District Attorney did not ask the identity of the "new" girl, and Leonard waived the right to question the witness.

When she did leave the stand, I broke my self-imposed rule not to look back at any of the spectators except my mother. I followed Elisa with my eyes as she walked back and sat down beside her husband. Something had banished his scowl. Maybe it was satisfaction over Manuelo's death.

At lunchtime I asked Leonard why it was that Elisa Dalton, out of all such possible witnesses, had been the one to appear on the stand.

"The D.A. goes after all the publicity he can get. And maybe Elisa Dalton could use the publicity too right now. I heard that she's being dropped from her TV series."

The next day both the District Attorney and Leonard rested their cases. The morning after that the D.A. gave his summation, calling for a verdict of first-degree, premeditated murder. Early in the afternoon, Leonard, in his final plea, called for my acquittal, on the grounds that the evidence against me was entirely circumstantial.

The jury was out only three hours. Their verdict was just what Leonard had predicted, murder in the second degree.

So perhaps his appeals to the sympathy of those twelve men and women had done some good. At least they had not decided upon premeditated murder.

Two weeks later I was returned to that same courtroom for sentencing. The judge gave me four to twelve years in the Tattinger Institute for Women.

As a uniformed woman led me toward the courtroom's side door, I turned my head to smile at my mother's white face. She tried to smile back, but didn't quite make it.

154

15

Like the county jail, prison turned out to be not nearly as bad as I had feared. In fact, Tattinger was the sort of prison—regularly denounced by some taxpayers—that tries to see to it that its "girls," when they leave, are a little better equipped to handle life than when they came in. There was a library as large as that in many a small town. Prisoners did not learn skills, such as hand-weaving, for which there was little demand in the outside world. Instead they mastered such work as cooking, typing, or bookkeeping. Food, much of it raised by the inmates, was plain but ample. We were housed not in cells, but in rooms with unbarred windows, and with only two girls to a room. There were even curtains, and unless you acquired too many demerits you could keep plants. What seemed most important of all to some of the inmates was that we did not have to wear uniforms. We could wear clothes that we had brought with us or ones that we had managed to buy out of the modest sums Tattinger paid us for our work.

I'm sure that some women at Tattinger

found themselves cleaner, better fed, and better housed than ever before in their lives.

But it was still a prison. Anytime I looked out through my unbarred window with its white curtain, I saw the high stone wall that surrounded the place.

What was more, I knew that because of my imprisonment here, my life was ruined.

Oh, I would survive. After I left here in four years—I was determined to do nothing to add to that minimum sentence—I would, no doubt, find life livable, even pleasant at times. But mine would not be a normal existence, with marriage or children. How could I, a convicted murderer, inflict upon a child the terrible burden of calling me mother?

From the first, though, I tried to make the best of my situation. Given my choice of starting in the laundry room or kitchen, I chose the kitchen and actually took a certain pleasure in all that stainless-steel equipment. And I liked my roommate. (She was the first of several I had; for reasons known only to itself, the administration kept shifting us around.) Her name was Donna Jeanne, and she and her boyfriend had driven a stolen truck filled with cigarette cartons clear from Tampa to Boston before getting caught.

We were allowed visitors once a week. Mr. Burford, who had loaned my mother the money for my lawyer, also gave her time off to visit me. She and I would sit in the visiting room, quite a nice room, filled with rattan furniture with cretonne-covered cushions, which some rich woman had donated. Always, a matron was present, seated behind a table at one end of the room. She was out of earshot, especially if the inmates and visitors kept their voices down, but she maintained a close watch. At some times Tattinger seemed something like a very strict boarding school. But where visitors were concerned, the administration never lost sight of the fact that this was a prison for felons, and that their friends and family members might try to smuggle them guns or knives or drugs.

My mother and I chattered brightly during her visits, and smiled a great deal. She did not fool me, and I doubt that I fooled her, but I think the pretense helped us both.

I had been at Tattinger eight months when I was told, at mid-morning one visiting day, that I had a caller. Usually my mother did not arrive until late afternoon. Puzzled, I left my pile of pots and pans and hurried toward the visitors' room.

It was not my mother, but a vaguely familiar-looking girl my own age. After a moment I cried, "Why, Bobbie Sue! How wonderful!"

"Then you don't mind?"

"Mind! Here, let's sit down."

We sat facing each other on one of the rattan sofas. I had known Bobbie Sue Keeble all through Oresburg grammar school and the district high school, and yet I had never known her well. She was far from pretty. Coarse dark hair sprang from a low forehead. Her skin had been bad all through high school, and her cheeks still bore a few scars. But she had lovely hazel eyes, gentle and expressive.

She said, "I wasn't sure whether you'd— I mean, I always liked you in school, Sara, but you were so popular and all, that I was afraid to try to be your friend. Then I got to thinking that maybe now you might like it if I visited, and so I called up the pri— this place and asked about visiting days."

My throat tightened. No one else from high school or from the San Jimenez Academy of Music had been to see me or even written to me. I managed to say, "I'm so glad."

"Maybe you don't remember, but I'm

married. I married Joey Buskin, right after high school graduation."

I did not remember her marriage, but I did remember Joey Buskin, who also grew up in Oresburg. He was a nice boy, tall and shy, with big ears and big hands. The hands helped make him our star basketball player.

"Joey and I have a little boy. He's three months old now."

"Oh, that's wonderful!"

We talked for nearly an hour, mostly about Oresburg and about high school. With a tact that made me wish we had become friends a long time ago, she asked not a single question about the prison, or about my trial.

When she got up to leave she asked, "Okay if I visit you again?"

"Oh, please. Visit as often as you can."

"I don't see why I can't get down here once a month. I can leave little Joey with my mother, catch the early bus down here, and get home in time to make dinner. Or if I take later buses Joey and little Joey can have dinner with Mama."

She did visit me after that at least once a month, sometimes a little more often. Those months stretched into a year, a year and a half. I discovered that, at least for me, imprisonment did strange things to one's sense

159

of time. At first it had seemed to crawl. Later, perhaps because of monotonous prison routine, with each day almost exactly like the one before, it seemed to speed up.

I discovered something else, too. I no longer loved Manuelo. For a little while before his death, and for a longer while thereafter, I had hated him, but I was still in love. In love with the memory of his voice, his dark eyes, his well-muscled body. One day nearly a year after I came to Tattinger I discovered that was no longer true. All I felt was wonder that I could ever have loved a man who, despite his professional attainments, was essentially two years old. As with any two-year-old, all that had mattered to him was his own gratification. To attain it he would exploit without qualms the young, the inexperienced, the vulnerable.

Finding that his memory no longer held power over me seemed to have a liberating effect. Caged as I was, I tried to make my day-to-day life as rich as possible. I asked for, and received, permission to transfer to a job in the prison library. Twice a week, between suppertime and lights out, I played for my fellow inmates on the slightly out-of-tune upright in the rec room. I took the typing and computing courses the prison of-

160

fered. And whenever someone from the outside delivered a lecture, I always attended, even if the subject was something that didn't particularly interest me, like American Indian pottery.

I had been imprisoned at Tattinger two and a half years when the film department at nearby UCLA offered to help the Tattinger inmates make a short experimental movie. I doubt that all of us would have reacted so enthusiastically had the proposed film been a documentary about our daily life at Tattinger. But it was to have a real story, based on a medieval folk tale about some people from ancient Cathay, or China, whose wanderings somehow brought them to a tiny European village. All the roles, those of men as well as women, would be played by Tattinger inmates. And although we would follow the rough outline of the story, we'd improvise much of our dialogue. Under the direction of people from the university, we would make our own costumes and even construct sets. The main outdoor set, representing the medieval village with its crude thatched huts, would be built near the vegetable garden.

I spent every moment possible sewing, hammering, and devising and revising my lines. (They were not many, because mine was a small role.) In a coarse black wig with a pigtail, dark contact lenses, and a long padded gown, I was one of the visitors from Cathay.

When the picture was finished the university people let us keep materials that would help us to put on plays or perhaps even make another movie—costumes, make-up, even the collapsible false fronts that represented the village. Sometime later, to the accompaniment of our laughter, applause, and occasional groans, the film was shown in the rec hall. That same evening a woman from the university announced that our film might even make a little money. No major TV network wanted it, of course, but some local stations had expressed an interest. Once expenses had been deducted, any TV money left over would be given to the Tattinger recreation fund.

More months passed. My mother never missed a visiting day, and Bobbie Sue still came to see me once a month or so. The third anniversary of my incarceration at Tattinger came, and, several months later, the twenty-fourth anniversary of my birth. I felt much older than that. Sometimes, looking in the mirror, I felt surprised that I still appeared so young.

But if I felt much older and harder inside, I also felt stronger, more capable of handling whatever happened to me in the future. One thing that helped my self-confidence was that I had achieved my goal of a perfect record, with no demerits whatsoever. As a result, I had been made what in old-style prisons is called a trusty, but here was called a "privileged." As such, I was sometimes given duties that took me outside the prison walls. I drove into the small town nearby to borrow books from their library for our own. In the case of an inmate or staff member who needed medical attention not available in the Tattinger infirmary, I drove the patient into town to a clinic or a doctor's office and waited outside to drive us both back to prison.

Those brief excursions outside the high gray walls did more than anything else to sustain me during my remaining time at Tattinger. Soon I would be part of that world, where people moved freely along the sidewalks and in and out of stores, theaters, restaurants, whatever places they chose to visit. True, my four years here would have closed to me the possibility of certain kinds of happiness, such as having children, or perhaps even marrying. Would any man—or at least any man I would want to marry—consider taking a convicted murderer as a wife?

But my world could hold other satisfactions. Probably I could always earn a living playing the piano one place or another. And thanks to classes I had taken here, I had other saleable skills. I could operate a computer and accurately type sixty words a minute.

The only deeply troubling aspect of my last months at Tattinger was my mother. Plainly the cumulative effect of my imprisonment was turning out to be far harder on her than on me. Each time I saw her she seemed paler, thinner, older. Well, my release would bring back the color to that still pretty face of hers. More than ever, I was determined not to mar my record in any way, lest the authorities have an excuse to hold me beyond my minimum sentence.

I had less than six months left to serve when one of the girls who acted as monitor came into the library one morning. "Sara, you've got a visitor. It's that friend of yours."

I felt surprise. Bobbie Sue must have caught the earliest bus. For the past several months she had been making her visits at the same time as my mother, so that they could ride back and forth together. I turned over the catalogue file I had been working on to my helper, a newly arrived girl serving one year for attempted grand larceny, and hurried to the visiting room.

"Hello, Sara." Bobbie Sue's smile was wide, too wide.

"Didn't Mother come with you?"

"No, she couldn't."

"What do you mean, couldn't?"

"Don't look like that, Sara. Everything's all right. Let's sit down and I'll tell you."

We sat on one of the rattan sofas. "It's her job. You know that a San Francisco company has bought into the mine, don't you?"

"I didn't know, and anyway, what's that to do with my mother?"

"The—the new people don't want to go on giving her a day off in the middle of the week. Look, Sara," she rushed on, "it means her job! And anyway, you'll be out soon, only another six months."

"You're lying to me, Bobbie Sue!"

"Lying to you? Why should I lie?"

"What's happened to my mother?" I had spoken so loudly and fiercely that the matron at the other end of the room looked at me.

I said, lowering my voice, "You tell me the truth, Bobbie Sue, or I'll slap you silly."

Her face crumpled. "I knew I couldn't fool you. Joey said I couldn't. But she made me promise—Oh, Sara! Your mom's sick. She's awfully sick."

After a long moment I said, "Cancer?"

She nodded.

"Where?" I knew I had to get the important question out before my throat closed entirely.

"The—the pancreas."

"How long?"

"How long has she got to—The doctors say four months, maybe five."

"Where is she?"

"She—she moved out of that apartment. She's in the house in the woods. She wants to stay there as long as she can."

It was February now. Here near the southern California coast winters were kind. But farther north, and at Oresburg elevation, February could be cruel indeed, and even crueler in that house in the woods. There was no heat in it except for the wood-and-coal stove in the kitchen and a small fireplace in the little parlor.

As if reading my mind, Bobbie Sue said, "People will bring her groceries and firewood." She tried to smile. "And she's got Charlie with her."

Charlie, who must have become a very elderly dog indeed by now.

I could see why she wanted to spend her last months in that woodland house rather than in a cramped apartment above the hardware store. In the house she would feel closer to her happy young self, closer to my father, closer to me when I was little.

"Please, Sara. Please send her a letter. Just make like you believed me. Just say you understand about her new boss, and that anyway you'll be out in less than six months."

"All right."

"And when I get home from here today I'll tell her you believed me."

"All right."

She put her hand on my arm. "Please, please, Sara. Don't try anything foolish. I mean, Joey knows something about state prison rules. His uncle was a guard at Folsom. There's not much chance they'll let you out to stay with her. So please, Sara—"

"All right." I got to my feet. "I'd like to be alone now, Bobbie Sue."

She also stood up. I said, "I didn't mean that about slapping you silly. I love you, Bobbie Sue."

167

"I know." She gave me a rigid smile and walked out of the room.

Half an hour later I sat with the warden in her office. She said, "I'm sorry, Sara. I really mean that. I've come to like you and respect you. I can give you compassionate leave, yes, but only when your mother is *in extremis*. Do you know what that means?"

"Dying."

"Yes. Try to look at this from the state's point of view. No matter what the provocation, the fact remains that you took another human being's life."

"A jury said I did."

"Yes, and that's all the state has to go on, isn't it? Now you owe the state a minimum of four years. Not three and a half. Four. And suppose we did allow you to go to your mother now. Unless we sent guards, at the taxpayers' expense, to watch you twenty-four hours a day, how could we be sure that you would come back to serve the rest of your sentence?

"Those are the reasons behind the rule, Sara. Now try to take what comfort you can in the thought that her doctor might be mistaken. They sometimes are, you know. She might live for quite a while after your sentence is finished. Why, there's even such a thing as permanent remission."

"Yes. May I go now, Warden?"

She nodded. "But just one more thing. Don't even contemplate doing something . . . . foolish. If you did, you probably would find yourself serving a much longer sentence. At the very least, you'd have to serve the maximum they gave you. Twelve years, wasn't it? And it might well be in one of the old-style prisons. Believe me, they're not like Tattinger. All right, you can go now."

I finished my day in the library. I ate supper. I read in my room until lights out. Then, while my roommate snored gently in the other bed, I stared into the darkness and planned how I was going to break out of Tattinger.

16

The next morning, wearing a denim skirt with oversized pockets, I went to the storeroom off the rec room. There, among the collapsible Ping-Pong tables, Scrabble sets, and jigsaw puzzles, were several large boxes of props left to us by the experimental film group. I took what I needed and then reported to the library.

During lunch break I went to my room, packed a beige canvas tote bag, and placed it far back in my closet. No one would wonder about my carrying a tote bag out of Tattinger. When on official assignments outside the walls, a "privileged" was allowed to make purchases.

Still on my lunch break, I went to the matron who acted as prison bursar and drew out three hundred dollars of my savings "for a stereo." I longed to draw out every cent, but dared not. It would have been a clear signal of my intent. Tight-lipped with disapproval—she had often praised me for "the nice little nest egg" I was accumulating—she doled out the cash in twenties.

No sooner had I resumed my work in the library than I was struck with the bleak conviction that I had messed everything up right at the start. In view of my interview with the warden, and my withdrawal of the money, would they let me proceed with my next day's assignment outside the prison walls? It seemed to me now that the answer was no. They would either give my assignment to someone else, or send a matron or another privileged along to watch me.

Perhaps I should never have withdrawn any money. But then, how could I have hoped to get along on the outside for even twenty-four hours without money?

I would just have to allay suspicion as best I could.

Late in the afternoon I went back to the bursar, handed her the three hundred, and asked her to keep it for me for another week. "I'm afraid I won't be able to buy that stereo tomorrow."

"Why not?"

"I don't think I'll be going outside. I feel as if I'm coming down with something. And I don't want to leave that money lying around in my room for a week."

She said, as if regaining some of her good opinion of me, "That's sensible of you." She scrutinized my face. "You do look pale. Best get over to the infirmary right away. It's the flu season, and it's especially bad this year. We don't want the whole place coming down with it."

"First I'll have to tell the warden—"

"I'll tell her someone will have to fill your assignment tomorrow." She reached for the phone. "Now get yourself over to the infirmary."

As I left her office I thought, that ought to do it. Surely the warden would not think I bore watching, not after I'd *asked* for release from that assignment.

At the infirmary I was given antihistamine tablets and instructions to drink lots of water, go to bed right after supper, and report back the next day if I did not feel better.

Of all my many weeks at Tattinger, the one that followed was the longest. Again and again as I catalogued new books in the library, or sat at meals in the noisy messhall, or lay awake in the dark, I felt a cold certainty that I still wouldn't get away with it. My assignment to the outside would be cancelled. Perhaps I would not be allowed beyond the walls again, not until I'd served the remaining months of my sentence, or until my mother, in the warden's phrase, was *in extremis*, perhaps unable to understand me, even recognize me . . .

To keep from crying out, and thus arousing my roommate, I would put my hand around my throat and press with my fingers.

The afternoon before my usual day to go outside, I went to the bursar and again drew out three hundred dollars. Perhaps glad that

I hadn't introduced flu into the prison, she gave me the money without comment. I repacked the tote bag I had unpacked the week before. That night I lay sleepless until past two o'clock.

There was no last-minute cancellation of my assignment, nor did they send anyone along to watch me! I don't know why. Perhaps my returning the money *had* allayed suspicion. Perhaps there had been no suspicion. Perhaps the warden had felt that in wanting a stereo I had been following that time-honored feminine prescription: when in emotional pain, buy yourself a present. Or perhaps she felt she had convinced me that I would be a fool to attempt an escape that, inevitably, would add years to my sentence.

All I know is that early the next morning the Tattinger gates opened and I drove one of the prison cars, a gray Chevrolet, onto the sunrise-reddened street. Beside me was the prison's kitchen supervisor, a Mrs. Dudley. Several months earlier she had fallen and broken her hip, and since her release from the hospital she had been going into town for physical therapy once each week. As we moved through the almost empty streets she chatted about her newest grandson. Heartbeat rapid, I tried not to say too much or too little, tried not to clutch the wheel too hard, lest she find my behavior different than on all those other mornings I had driven her into town.

I stopped before the clinic, a modest frame building on a residential street lined with smooth-barked eucalyptus trees. I said, "I think I'll do a little window shopping while you are in there."

"Do that." She got out and reached behind the front seat for her cane. I did not offer to help her to the clinic door. Going up the walk and climbing the three steps to the porch was part of her therapy.

Before she even reached the porch, I had eased away from the curb. I drove straight through the little town, then turned onto the highway that led to Bellford, a larger town. A mile or so before I reached Bellford, I turned into a service station. Apparently I was the first customer of the day. The attendant was just unlocking the glass-fronted office.

"Fill 'er up?" he asked.

I knew that the Chevrolet, free of any sort of official insignia, could not be identified as a prison vehicle unless someone saw the registration slip. Nevertheless, I could hear tension in my voice as I said, "Yes, please. And is there a ladies' room?"

"I'll give you the key."

The restroom was around the corner of the building. I went into the cement-floored room and closed the door, praying that no one would come in for the next ten minutes or so. If I did hear someone outside, what should I do? Gather up my gear, dart into one of cubicles, and stay there until she had left? Yes, that was about all I could do.

I reached into my tote bag and, from beneath the clothing I had stuffed into it, brought out the materials I had taken from the rec room storage closet the week before. I took off my dark glasses, untied the printed cotton scarf with which I'd covered my head, then verified the label on the spray can of hair dye, the kind that shampooing will remove. Yes, it was "sable brown" rather than the "ebony" I'd used for my role in the film. As rapidly as I could, I sprayed my hair until it was dripping wet, soaked up some of the moisture with a paper towel, then combed the dye through.

The contact lenses, in a small cardboard box with my name still on it, were also brown. The box also held a vial of contact lens solution, which I used before slipping the lenses into place. I looked at myself in the mirror. Instead of a blue-eyed blonde, here stood a brown-eyed brunette, with wet hair. I replaced my head scarf and dark glasses and left.

As he took my money and made change, the attendant seemed to notice nothing different about me. Why should he have? A young woman wearing dark glasses and a head scarf had gone into the rest room and then emerged still wearing them.

I drove through Bellford and then took the thruway north.

It was jammed with work-bound traffic. When the streams of cars slowed to a bumper-to-bumper crawl, I looked at my watch. Was it late enough by now for Mrs. Dudley to have telephoned the prison? Yes, it was almost nine, more than late enough.

The traffic had picked up speed as cars peeled off at various exits. I tried to keep up without going too far over the legal limit. It would be ironic indeed if some speed cop—

Sirens back there somewhere. Heart beating a tattoo in my chest, I crowded with the other cars into the right lane. Two police cars, sirens still screaming, sped past and kept going. Shakily, I followed the car ahead of me into the passing lane.

A sign up ahead: LOS CERRITOS, NEXT EXIT.

I maneuvered over into the right lane. I had intended to get at least twenty miles farther away from the prison before leaving the thruway. But my nerves were too shaky for thruway driving. Chances were excellent that I would have an accident, and any accident, no matter how minor, was sure to land me back in Tattinger.

Besides, I'd heard that Los Cerritos had grown into a fair-sized city. Probably it would do as well as anywhere. All I needed was someplace to hide for about three weeks. Surely by then the authorities would have relaxed their watch on that house in the woods.

I took the Los Cerritos exit.

Near the point where the exit ramp joined the highway was an outdoor phone booth. I stopped. Inside the booth I dropped a coin, dialed, and at the operator's instruction dropped more coins. Through howls that I knew must be young Joey's, I heard Bobbie Sue say, "Hello."

"It's Sara."

"How are you, Sara?" Already her voice was thin with apprehension.

"Listen to me. Listen carefully. I've left Tattinger."

"Oh, Sara! Oh, *Sara!*" Then: "Where are you?"

"It's better that you don't know. And don't tell anyone you've heard from me. No one but my mother."

"She'll *know* you left. It'll be on TV, radio."

"I know. That's why you must tell her this. Now listen, Bobbie Sue. You tell her that I asked the warden for a compassionate leave of several months. She said it couldn't be given to me, not officially. But at the same time she hinted that—well, that if I just drove away and laid low for a while, nothing too bad would happen to me, not if I came back to serve the rest of my sentence."

"Oh, Sara! Is that true? Did the warden really—"

"Never mind if it's true. Just convince my mother of it, that's all. Do you think you can?"

"I don't know. But at least she'll *want* to believe it."

"Convince her of it. Tell her I'll see her in about three weeks. And tell her she's not

178

to tell the police or *anyone* that she's heard from me, directly or indirectly. That goes for you too, of course."

"Oh, I realize that—"

"Goodbye, Bobbie Sue. I'm more grateful to you than I'll ever be able to say." I hung up, got back in the Chevrolet.

Soon I was driving between almost solid rows of new-and used-car lots and fast-food places. surely Los Cerritos must have residential districts, too. I made a left turn and found myself driving through streets lined with small houses, each with a luxuriantly planted front lawn. After the deafening thruway and the noisy highway, these empty streets seemed eerily quiet.

I parked the Chevrolet before a vacant lot on an otherwise fully developed street. I took all the papers from the glove compartment and crammed them without looking at them into my tote bag. Now there were no documents in the car to identify it as prison property.

At the corner I turned and walked left, back toward the highway. Soon I was aware of a tall sign revolving against the blue, late-morning sky. From that distance I could not tell whether it advertised a motel, a car lot, or a restaurant.

I walked toward it, not knowing that it was leading me to Sammy's half-priced and wholly appalling meals, and my ten-dollar motel room, and my saturnine yet somehow likable landlord.

17

I had been in Los Cerritos almost two weeks when the gray Chevrolet disappeared.

I stood motionless on the corner. During my several trips to that intersection, the presence of the car had come to seem like a reassuring symbol of something—my own good luck, say, or the ineptitude of the police. Now I felt a leap of panic.

I walked quickly away, thinking of how in one of those small neat houses someone might be at the phone. "Yes, she's been back, the one who's come to the corner several times and looked down the street at the car. She's walking away now."

I had an absurd impulse to break into a run. I checked it. After a few moments I began to think more clearly. Even if someone had noticed my coming to that corner a few times, it was unlikely that he or she would connect me with that car, just because I had looked briefly down the street where it was parked.

And even if the police, rather than some thief, had taken the Chevy away, it did not necessarily mean that my peril had increased. True, it would not take them long to identify it as the car I had driven away from Tattinger. But it was almost equally certain that they would make only the most cursory search of this neighborhood. They would assume that by now I had put many miles between myself and that abandoned car. Nevertheless, it was with the sense of some hunted animal reaching its den that I entered my motel room—a quiet one now, because those painters and carpenters had finished their job two days before. I locked the door and flung myself across the bed.

If only more time had passed since my escape. If only I felt it reasonably safe now to buy a junky old car from one of those lots and start driving north toward that house in the piney woods, that house where my mother had chosen to spend the last—

My mother. For the first time it struck me that, in my frustration and grief, I might actually have added to my mother's suffering.

What if Bobbie Sue had not been able to

convince her that the authorities had tacitly acquiesced to my escape? If that were the case, then she was bearing a double burden now, her physical suffering plus the conviction that her daughter almost inevitably would remain not just another six months in prison but much, much longer.

And that, of course, would be the case. When I returned to Tattinger I might have to serve out my maximum sentence, twelve years. I had realized that even as I made my plans to escape. But if that was the price I eventually would have to pay, so be it. For me the only important consideration was that my mother not spend those last weeks of her life apart from me, the one person she had left to love.

But now I looked at the situation from her point of view. Unless Bobbie Sue had managed to convince her that I would be all right, she might at this moment be picturing me back in prison. She might be thinking of how I would emerge at thirty-two or -three, my youth irretrievably lost—

I must get in touch with Bobbie Sue, try to learn whether or not she had convinced my mother. I had an impulse to rush to the nearest pay phone. But no. I must think carefully about what I was to say. Doubtless by now the police had tapped Bobbie Sue's phone, knowing that she was the one person besides my mother who had visited me in prison. And that presented me with two problems. I would have to make our contact brief, in the hope of being able to hang up before the police traced the call. And I would have to phrase my questions so as to elicit from Bobbie Sue the maximum amount of information in the minimum of time.

I looked at my watch. Almost five. At six Mike and I were supposed to go to a Mexican restaurant, "someplace really different," near the ocean. A man named Dave Winninger, who was interested in buying the motel, would take over at the desk until the night man came on.

Given my heightened fear of the police and my newfound doubts about my conduct these past two weeks, I had a desire to stay huddled on the bed. But that was foolish. If by some wild chance the police right now were searching for me in Los Cerritos, they would find me as easily in this motel room as in some restaurant. And as for my anguished doubts about what my conduct might have done to my mother, I could not resolve that until I had made a carefully thought-out phone call to Bobbie Sue.

183

For right now, best to keep that dinner date. I got out of bed and undressed for the shower.

The restaurant was in an old Mexican farmhouse, set in a field of commercially grown flowers. The fragrance of lavender and spicy carnations filled the gathering dark as we drove down a badly potholed road. PEDRO'S, a blue neon sign in front of the farmhouse announced. Then, in smaller letters: HOME OF THE TWO-HUNDRED-YEAR-OLD GRAPEVINE.

"That two hundred years may be a slight exaggeration," Mike said, "but it's plenty old and plenty big. You'll see."

Because the night was mild, the management had decided to open the outdoor part of the restaurant. Small tables sat beneath the grapevine, an awesome growth of huge leaves and thick, twisted branches that, held up by wooden supports, formed a roof at least fifty feet square. There was no noisy mariachi, no stereo; just a guitarist and accordionist, both middle-aged, who sat beside a tiny dance floor and played plaintive songs from south of the border.

It was while we were drinking our predinner tequila that I looked up from my glass and, with a sense of shock, met Mike's unsmiling gaze. In that moment I realized that he felt more than liking for me, quite a lot more. I learned, too, that there was something profoundly troubled in his feeling for me.

And as our eyes held, I discovered something about myself. My emotion for him was also a good deal more than liking, more than gratitude for a room I could afford, and for shared dinners and talk.

I asked myself that most bootless of questions. *Why hadn't this happened four years ago?* Why hadn't I met this decent, straightforward young guy back in the days when I had no idea how ugly and brutal the world could be? Because it was too late now. I couldn't love him. I had no right to fall in love with anyone.

The musicians began to play a familiar waltz, "La Golondrina."

"Don't you dance?" I asked swiftly.

"More or less. Would you like to?"

I had been right. On the dance floor, even with his hand clasping mine and his arm around me, I felt less of that troubling intimacy than I had with his eyes looking deep into mine.

We left before ten and drove through the fragrant dark to the not-so-fragrant highway.

Mike walked me to my motel room. No brotherly kiss on the cheek tonight. Instead he said, "Good night, Sara," kissed me hard but briefly on the mouth, and walked away.

I went into the room and switched on the light. Why hadn't he tried to stay with me longer, when he obviously wanted to? But I mustn't think about him. Probably, after I left here, I would never see him again. All I should think about now was that phone call to Bobbie Sue.

It was five o'clock the next day before I felt I had planned my call as well as I possibly could. I did not make it from the motel, of course, or even one of the nearby public phones. Instead, just on the chance that I might not be able to get off the line before the call was traced, I took the bus several miles to that shopping mall, and made the call from there.

She answered on the second ring. I said, "You know who this is? Did you do what I asked?"

I felt sweat on my upper lip. This was the moment of truth. If she cried out my name or began to dither, I'd just have to hang up and walk away as rapidly as possible.

In a voice so strained it sounded hoarse, she said, "Yes, I told her."

"Did she believe you?"

"I think so. Maybe it was just because she wanted so much to believe, but I think she did. But oh, Sa—"

She checked herself and then went on, "I'd almost rather die than tell you this. But listen to me. It's been awfully cold here. Snowing a lot. Charlie must have gotten out."

Charlie, that old dog who hadn't been too bright even as a young one. I felt numb, almost as if I already knew the whole story.

"It was one night last week. She must have gone looking for him. They found her around noon the next day, almost covered with snow. Later they found Charlie a few yards away, entirely covered up. That's how they knew she must have been looking for him when she tripped or something. Anyway, she was—she was—"

Death by freezing. Someone had called it "one of death's kindest faces." You just get drowsy and fall asleep and stay that way. Certainly it was kinder than what had awaited her. I must keep thinking that, keep thinking that, keep thinking that.

"Where? When?"

Obviously Bobbie Sue had anticipated that I would call. Probably she had talked it over with Joey and decided how to answer the questions I would be likely to ask.

"In the churchyard."

Only one church in Oresburg, the Congregational.

"But oh, Sa—It was held two days ago."

So there had been no chance of going to her funeral—even if, with the police sure to be there waiting for me, I nevertheless had decided to go. I hung up. I leaned against the booth wall for a moment and then left.

On my way back in the bus, with its sparse load of the infirm, the very young, and the very old, I wondered dully why there had been nothing about my mother's death in the newspapers or on TV. Her death was newsworthy. She had been the mother of an escapee from a state prison, a girl who had been convicted after a highly publicized trial.

The answer came to me. The police had asked that the news be withheld. They must still have been watching the house in the woods, still have been hoping that I would show up there.

From the bus stop I walked through the brief southern California twilight to the motel. I let myself into the darkened room and turned on the light.

The phone rang.

It was Mike. "I've called you a couple of times. How would you like to go to that Mexican place again tonight?"

I had to force the words out. "No, thank you. I don't feel well. A very bad headache."

"Look, I've got some new medicine for that. Let me bring it up."

"I've got medicine. Thank you, Mike. But I'd rather just rest. Good night."

I hung up, turned off the light, and fell onto the bed. I wanted to howl, like an animal in agony. But I found out something then. When you're alone, utterly alone, you don't cry. It must be that tears are a form of communication, a way of asking someone who loves you to share your pain. And when there is no one—

I just lay there, hands clutching the pillows, while memories of her tore at me.

A knock at the door. I lay rigid. Another knock. "Sara?" Mike's voice.

The rattle of a key in the lock. I heard the door open, felt the rush of cool night air. I said, in a voice I myself scarcely recognized, "Don't turn on the light."

"All right." He came over to the bed, sat down. "What is it, Sara? What's happened?"

"My mother—" I could not force more words out of my throat.

189

"What happened to your mother?"

"She went out looking for Char—for our old dog. It was snowing. She must have fallen, must have been too—too weak to get up—"

He said, after several moments, "Then your mother has died."

I gasped, "Yes."

He lay down beside me, gathered me close. "Cry," he commanded. "Cry."

The tears came in a flood. For a time there was no sound in the room except my convulsive sobs.

When at last I lay quiet he said, "All right. Now tell me about it. Not just your mother. All of it."

I lay speechless in his arms.

"Maybe it would help you to talk if you knew that I already know a lot about you. You're not Sara Blanding. You're Sara Hargreaves, aren't you?"

After a long while I said, "How did—"

"I first saw you almost four years ago. I was studying pre-law at UCLA then. I became so interested in your case that one day I cut classes and went up to your trial. You were on the stand. You were so pitiful. All this circumstantial evidence against you. And all you could keep saying was that you hadn't killed him. The funny part was that I found myself believing you. My reaction almost embarrassed me. Here I was, a pre-law student, already with some training in the rules of evidence, and yet I was believing *you*.

"I saw you again only about a year ago, or rather, your image on film. I was working for that Los Angeles brokerage house then. One night I had dinner at the house of an old UCLA friend. He said that an experimental film made by the university's film department was going to be shown on a local channel, so after dinner we watched it. One of the Chinese characters looked familiar, in spite of shiny black hair that looked dyed, and eyes taped at the corners to give them a slant. When the credits rolled, there was the name, Sara Hargreaves.

"And so, when you walked into my office that morning and registered as Sara Blanding, I felt I knew pretty sure who you were, in spite of the fact that the dark hair showing beneath your scarf was not as dark as it had been in the film, and your eyes weren't slanted. When I heard the first news broadcast about your escape, that clinched it."

"And yet you didn't call the police," I

said, in a voice hoarse from prolonged weeping.

"No."

After a moment he went on. "Tell me about this Miguel Covarrubias."

"Manuelo."

"Manuelo. Tell me the whole thing, right from the beginning."

I tried to, but in my emotional and mental exhaustion I couldn't keep my story straight. I began with my arrival at Serena, then went back to my first sight of Manuelo at the Miraflores Inn in San Jimenez. Then, somehow, I had skipped ahead to the day I saw Manuelo with Gabriella Montgomery, that girl with the hauntingly lovely face.

Somehow, though, I finally got it all in. The Christmas Day party at Serena, Manuelo's bout with the flu, and my finding that damning statement about Dr. Swedenborg in the safe. And, the night before Manuelo's death, the sound of his quarrel with someone behind his closed apartment door.

A little more coherently now, I told him about Bobbie Sue's last visit to Tattinger, and about my phone call to her after I drove away in the prison car. "I came here, to wait until it would be safer to go to my mother's house. But when I phoned Bobbie Sue a few hours ago, she told me, she told me—"

His arms tightened around me. "What are you going to do now?"

"What is there to do," I asked dully, "except what I always planned to do after—after my mother died? I'll go back to Tattinger to serve out my sentence, and hope they won't add too much—"

"No! Don't you realize you may have to serve the maximum, at the very least? Eight more years, Sara!" He kissed me briefly. "Eight years! Perhaps even longer. After all, you did escape. And they may make you serve that time in a much tougher prison than Tattinger."

The warden had told me much the same thing.

He kissed me again, this time not briefly. My arms tightened around his neck. I experienced something I had never experienced before, nor expected to. Not just the beginning of desire, but tenderness, and sadness, and overwhelming gratitude, all mixed up.

"Sara?" he said, lips close to my ear.

"Yes," I said. "Yes, Mike."

When at last we lay quietly, my cheek against his bare chest, I realized that perhaps it was strange that in this tragic hour I could feel desire. And yet there had seemed to be something natural about it, something healing and life-affirming.

He smoothed The hair away from my face. "You see? This is one of the reasons you can't go back to prison for eight or even more years, or any fraction of that. I want you to spend those years with me."

And I wanted to spend them with him.

"Oh, Mike!" No one could know how horrifying to me was the thought of going back now. I thought of being shut away, perhaps for years, always wondering what Mike might be doing, whom he might have met. Oh, I knew that he would promise to wait. I knew that as surely as he was lying beside me now. But the waiting years could seem long to a man in a world full of lovely young women. . . .

I cried, "But what am I to do?"

"What are *we* to do," he corrected. "Right at the moment, I don't know. But I do know I could sell the motel immediately. We could go to Canada. They say it's easy to go abroad from there—"

"No! I don't want us to be wandering about, exiles from our own country. And I especially don't want it for you. You planned to be a lawyer, Mike! I want you to have what you planned."

I raised myself on one elbow. "Mike, do you believe I'm innocent, really innocent? Or do you feel I must have killed him in some strange kind of a fit, and then wiped it out of my memory?"

Arc light from the parking lot filtered through a crack between the two halves of the heavy draperies. I could see Mike's unsmiling face. "No." He reached up and touched my cheek. "Crazy as it might sound to some people, I don't believe you did it at all."

"You believe someone else did?"

"Obviously."

"Then don't you see, Mike? There is only one way I can ever really be free."

"I know," he said. "I've been thinking about that, not just tonight, but for days and days. We've really got just one hope—and that's to find out what really happened."

18

Even after Mike left me that night I lay awake for hours in the darkness, thinking of the plans we had made. Nevertheless, I managed to get to work on time the next morning. Mike and I had agreed that until we were ready to leave this place we had best stick to routine.

When my shift was ended I went to my room and, as usual, turned on a local TV channel. The young black woman who anchored the daytime news program spoke of a minor oil spill off the Santa Barbara coast. Then she said, kindling excitement in her voice, "This is just in. There has been a break in the Sara Hargreaves case. The gray Chevrolet in which the convicted murderess fled Tattinger Institute for Women has been found abandoned on a dirt road through an onion field, three miles north of the Los Cerritos city limits. That is all the information we have at present."

I clutched the edge of the counter on which the TV stood. So it was not the police who had moved the car from where I had left it. It must have been thieves. Kids, probably. But why, oh why, hadn't they driven it north to San Francisco or south to San Diego? Why had they abandoned it only a few miles from this motel room?

Would the authorities conclude that I was somewhere nearby? Not necessarily. Nevertheless, the police in this area would be on the double alert.

How I wished I could turn to Mike right at that moment! But just as we had planned the night before, he was out looking for an RV to rent, or, if the price was low enough, to buy.

At seven I went down to his apartment. As I entered the living room, he walked in from the kitchen. He said, after a quick look at my face, "I know. I had the car radio on. Try not to worry too much. The police around here will be on a sharper lookout, of course, but they're not going to spare the manpower to fine-comb the whole area. Probably it was kids who took the Chevy from where you left it."

"I thought of that, too."

"There may be evidence it was kids. There usually is. Empty beer cans in the car, that sort of thing. And as far as the police know, they could have driven the car to that field from almost any place.

"And anyway," he added, "we should be out of here in a couple of days."

The office phone rang. He walked past me and through the office doorway. I heard him say, "Office," and then, after an interval, "All right, Mr. Stubbs. I'll be right up."

197

He walked back to me. "Guy in one-four-teen says the metal stopper in his bathtub won't fall into place. I should be back in a few minutes."

"Is there anything I can—"

"No. The salad's made, and the roast chicken is in the oven. Turn on the stereo —I just put in a Vivaldi tape—and try to relax."

When he had gone, I did turn on the music. Then I walked over to his bookshelves. It was the first time I had really looked at them. Law books occupied one whole shelf. The others held a mixture of fiction and non-fiction. I saw that he must be a World War II buff because there were several histories and novels concerned with it. And there were at least two books written by the sort of men Mike admired, lawyer-journalists. From their titles, I knew that one had been written by a D.A. who prosecuted a famous serial killer, and the other by a lawyer who had at first befriended a doctor accused of murdering his wife and children, and later turned evidence against the accused over to the police.

Mike needed at least one more bookshelf. The books in this one were packed too tightly. I tugged at a volume at one end of the shelf—Shaw's *The Young Lions*—until it came free. With it came a notebook that, unnoticed by me, had been wedged in between the Shaw novel and the side of the shelf. It fell, pages spreading, face down onto the floor.

I laid *The Young Lions* on the end table beside the sofa and picked up the notebook. It was the sort of notebook, with lined pages and stiff cardboard covers, that high school and college students use. Its outspread pages were covered with strong, back-slanted handwriting in pen and ink. I was about to close the notebook and put it back on the shelf when my own name seemed to leap out at me.

A partial sentence at the top of the left-hand page read, ". . . fast-food restaurant hired Sara Hargreaves as soon as she applied."

With hands that felt suddenly cold, I turned to the front of the notebook and then leafed slowly through it. It was all about me, and not just from the time I came to the motel. He had started his account with his attendance at my trial. Then he had written, "After her conviction and sentencing, I knew nothing of her except that she and other Tattinger inmates had acted in an experimental film, which I saw. Then, last February 11, she suddenly appeared at my motel."

He had written down everything, everything I had done and said in the past two weeks. As for what I had told him as I lay, sometimes weeping, in his arms the night before, it was all there. I pictured him kissing me for one last time as he sat on the edge of my bed, and then coming down here to write half the night in this notebook.

Why? I asked myself numbly. Why had he been compiling secretly this—this dossier about me? Well, I could imagine one reason, I thought with sudden cold bitterness. Or rather, a half million or more reasons. Surely that lawyer's account of how he had befriended an accused man, and then joined the prosecution, must have brought him at least a half million in book and TV rights.

With this pain twisting inside me, I wanted to race up to 114 and confront him. Either that or run out into the night and just keep going. But I must not. If Mike did not love me, if he was "helping" me only for his own selfish reasons, then I was truly alone. And when you're alone, when you really have no one but yourself to depend upon, you can't afford to give your emotions free rein. You have to try to think coldly, clearly, calmly.

I thrust *The Young Lions* and the notebook back onto the shelf. Then I sat down on the sofa and clasped my hands tightly in my lap.

This was no time, I decided, to demand an explanation of his actions. Unless he could give me a satisfactory one—and I could not imagine what such an explanation would be—everything between us would end right now, and in bitterness. And I needed him. True, I had needed him last night, I thought, with an anguished memory of tenderness and desire and trusting gratitude. But that was a different sort of needing. The need I had in mind now was merely my survival.

And probably Mike, no matter what his motives, would help me to survive, help me to keep from going back to prison. Why not, I thought cynically. It would make him seem even more of a hero in that book he was preparing.

True, if his main interest in me was that book, he might betray me if the going got really rough. He might walk out on me, or even make an anonymous phone call to the police. But I had to take that chance. What was my alternative? To cut and run all by

201

myself, just at a time when the police in the Los Cerritos area had been put on a heightened alert?

I thought of Manuelo. And now Mike. Was I the victim type, the sort of woman who is subconsciously attracted to the sort of man who will deceive her, make a fool of her? I had never thought of my being like that, but perhaps I was.

I was still sitting there, hands clenched in my lap, when Mike returned.

"Well, I fixed it. Had to go down to the storeroom for a wrench, but it's fixed." He broke off. "What is it? Still worrying about the cops finding that car?"

I managed to say, "Yes."

"Well, don't. As I told you, the odds that they'll come poking around this motel have gone up only a little. Anyway, we ought to be gone in a couple of days. Now let's have dinner and then talk some more about our plans."

19

The moonlit road, narrow and winding, led upward. Under the tires of our lumbering RV, occasional patches of ice crackled. We were in my California now, the California of pines, of deep snow turned blue by moonlight, of night birds that flew across the road as silently as shadows.

We had spent three days making our plans. Mike had told Dave Winninger, the prospective buyer of the motel, that he wanted to "take a break for a week or two, maybe longer." Would Winninger like to take over the place for that period? Eager to learn at first hand the pains and profits of the motel business, Winninger had agreed.

Yesterday Mike had rented the RV. It was far from new, but it had two worn leather seats that let down into beds, a small galley, and about everything else one would need for itinerant housekeeping. The manufacturer had even found room for a shower cubicle.

We had packed food and clothing last night so that we could get an early start. Before dawn we had pulled out of the motel parking lot and headed north. For about an hour we followed the coastal highway, with the long blue waves from China breaking on the beach below. Then we turned inland, traveling a series of roads that led north and east.

For a while I was dry-mouthed with anxiety. True, there had been no more TV bulletins about that gray Chevrolet, nor had police appeared at the motel. But I had an absurd sense that, like a cat at a mousehole, they might have been waiting for us to come out before they pounced. Twice the sound of a police siren brought the sweat out on my upper lip. But both times the police car sped past our slow-moving vehicle. Finally, I relaxed a little.

In the early afternoon we had a bit of bad luck. Something went wrong with the RV's feedline. The mechanic at a roadside garage had to send to the nearest town for a new part. Thus it was early evening before we got moving again. But now, at close to midnight, we were nearing Oresburg.

Mike had objected to our coming here. It was running an unnecessary risk, he said. I argued that the police would not be watching the churchyard, although they might have had someone there during my mother's funeral. But if they had listened to my last phone conversation with Bobbie Sue—and Mike agreed that it was almost certain they had—then they realized that I knew my mother was dead. They would feel I no longer had reason to come to this area.

"Besides," I said, "we won't even have to

go through Oresburg. The church is on the edge of town."

He gave in then, apparently realizing how much coming here meant to me. Or maybe he just grew tired of arguing. And so now, after an exhausting sixteen or seventeen hours—exhausting even though we had taken turns at the wheel—we were in an area familiar to me since early childhood, so familiar that I felt I could have walked this road blindfolded.

We rounded a curve. There was the church. Not one of those pretty white New England churches. The little mining town had built its church of native redwood. But it had a proper steeple, and a church yard with a split rail fence.

Mike waited in the RV while I opened the gate. The click of its latch was loud in the utter stillness. I stood motionless for a moment, but I sensed no watchers in the dark pines beyond the churchyard. I moved up the walk. It was treacherous underfoot. Evidently the path's snow covering had been trampled to a slush, and now the slush had frozen until it was as slippery as glass. But the snow on the grave mounds on either side of the path lay unblemished.

I knew where they would have placed

her—beside my father. There was nothing to show that her grave was only a few days old. The snow blanket made it look like all the others.

I stood there for several minutes, saying in my mind, Good-bye for now, Mother. Saying, I've got Mike, Mother. At least I think I've got him, at least for now, and so maybe everything is going to be all right.

My throat ached with tears, but I did not want to shed them until I was in Mike's arms. True, the shelter his arms offered was dubious now, but I needed it before I gave full sway to grief. Bending to the tombstone, I traced her newly carved name with my little finger on the cold marble. Then I went down the walk.

Mike drove the RV a few hundred yards and then pulled over to the side. He held me close while I wept.

When at last I was quiet we drove on for about a mile. Then, at my direction, he turned right onto a road so narrow that pine branches whipped the sides of our oversized vehicle. During the summer months young couples parked their cars here, and the night was filled with murmuring voices and giggles and the sound of low-tuned radios. But in winter the road was reclaimed by foxes and

206

deer, by small, furry creatures and the silent-winged night birds who hunted them.

Mike stopped the RV. Numb with fatigue, we dragged ourselves from the front seat back to the sleeping compartment.

20

Early the next afternoon, I said, "There's where you turn. See, just up ahead."

Mike turned the RV, not onto a road but just two tracks leading through the tall grass. When I had first walked these low, rounded hills, often with the voluble Patrick Murray beside me, the grass had been tawny yellow. Now winter rains had turned it emerald green, starred here and there with golden poppies.

When we had first begun to make our plans back in Los Cerritos, Mike had objected to our camping on Patrick Murray's land.

"But he'll never know about it," I said. "In all the times we walked together, he never accompanied me as far as that grove of live oaks, even though when I mentioned it he said he remembered where it was. It's at least two miles from that old carriage house where he lives, and about three miles from that bench where we used to sit, the one overlooking Serena. Besides—"

"Besides what?"

"It wouldn't matter if he did find out we were there. He's my friend."

"How do you know?"

"How do I know! Why, I told you. He put up a hundred fifty thousand dollars bail, so that I wouldn't have to stay in the county jail while my trial—"

"He knew you wouldn't skip your bail. Besides, what's a hundred fifty thousand to a rich man?" He paused. "Didn't it ever occur to you, Sara, that it might be conscience money?"

"Conscience money!" I stared at him, aghast. "You mean you think *Patrick* might have been the one who sneaked into Serena and knifed Manuelo in the back, and then framed—"

"Somebody did."

"But not Patrick! Oh, I don't say he didn't show every sign of wishing Manuelo as much bad luck as possible. But if he *had* killed him, he'd have used a gun, not a knife in the back. And then, if he saw the blame was being fastened on someone else, he would have turned himself in. He wouldn't have tried to frame me or anyone.

"Besides," I went on, "that grove is a perfect place to hide an RV. The grove can't even be seen from the road. And in the center of it there's a little spring, and a cleared space where somebody long ago must have built some sort of a shelter. Maybe it was only a tent house, since all I found were a few rotting boards. Think how much safer we'll be there than in some motor-home park or along the road somewhere. And yet it will be quite close to Serena."

In the end, we decided on the grove.

The RV moved on through the tall, poppy-strewn grass. How amazing this state is, I thought fleetingly. Less than two hundred miles to the east and north, where we had been only that morning, fir branches snapped beneath their burdens of snow. Less than two hundred miles to the south, subtropical plants and flowers bordered traffic-clogged highways. And it was all California.

We topped a rise. Below us was the grove of live oaks, some growing in the shallow depression, others straggling up the slope of the low hill opposite. Mike maneuvered the unwieldy vehicle on a winding course among the oaks and then stopped in the clearing.

We got out. While Mike raised the hood to look at the engine—it had been making odd noises again a few miles back—I walked over to the little spring that seeped from the hillside to trickle down into a quiet pool. I remembered the days when I used to come here. I had thought myself the luckiest girl alive, in love with Manuelo, and sure that he would be mine forever. Despite all the terrible things that had happened over those past four years, not for anything in the world would I have turned back the clock and become again that girl of almost twenty.

"What the hell are you doing here?"

I whirled around.

He had grown older and frailer-looking, but undoubtedly he was Patrick Murray. He even wore what looked like the same tweeds, plus the same chamois vest and cap. Only the blackthorn cane on which he leaned was new.

"This is my land! What are you doing on it?"

Struck dumb, I just stood there. A wrench in his hand, Mike also remained motionless.

Staring at me, Patrick Murray moved forward. "Sara?" Then he stopped short. "It *is* Sara." He didn't sound dismayed, or alarmed, or even particularly surprised. "But what have you done to your hair?"

"It's a rinse. It washes out."

"The saints be praised for that. I liked you better blond. And your eyes. Have I lost my wits, or were your eyes blue?"

"Were and are. These are contact lenses."

"I heard the news about you, and I thought, 'Maybe she'll come here, maybe she'll come to her old friend Patrick for help.'" Before I could reply to that, he turned to Mike. "And who might you be?"

"The name's Rolfe, Mike Rolfe."

"I've a Dublin cousin named Rolfe. Would you be Irish, then?"

"One of my great-grandfathers was." Patrick had stuck out his hand. Mike shook it. "But I hope it won't matter too much that he was an Orangeman."

Patrick shrugged. "All that's a long ways away, and in your great-grandfather's case a long time ago." He paused. "How is it you came here?"

"Sara remembered this grove from four years ago."

I said quickly, "We didn't mean to involve you, Mr. Murray. We didn't intend for you to even know about it. You see, I thought you never came to this part of your property."

"Didn't used to. But the doctor I have now says I must walk four miles a day. Walk! Doctors follow fads, same as everyone else. You come to a doctor with an infected hangnail these days and he'll say, 'What you need is to walk more.'"

He turned back to Mike. "Does that thing run?"

"Yes. The fan belt needed adjusting, that's all."

"Then let's all drive up to my place. I've had enough walking for one day."

Mike and I exchanged a long look. I could see he still had his doubts about this voluble man. But the die was cast now. Patrick Murray had seen us. Even if Mike hustled me into the RV and drove off, all the old man would have to do would be to phone our license number to the police.

I trusted him already, and Mike had no alternative. "Okay," he said.

He handed me into the high front seat, then helped Murray up. He got behind the wheel and, at Murray's direction, drove over the long grass to a narrow dirt road. Soon I saw the house. As we drew closer, I saw that four years had added to its ruination. The lowest of the broad steps leading up to the shadowy porch had caved in. On the second floor, shutters now hung askew. In fact, the place brought another comparison to mind —it looked like a set for a teenage horror movie.

When we drove around the corner of the old mansion, the carriage house looked spruce by comparison. Apparently even its gray paint had been renewed recently.

But the inside of the little house seemed as incongruous as ever, the massive and expensive old pieces of furniture from the mansion contrasting with the rough carriage-house flooring and the lean-to kitchen.

"First I'll give you some tea," said our host. "Then we'll talk."

He served the tea, a fragrant jasmine variety, in Spode cups that also must have come from the main house. To accompany it were lemon cookies, a little stale and hard, but edible.

At last he said, "All right, Sara. Why did you run away from that place, when you had only a few months left to serve?"

I told him about my mother.

He reached across the wide old mahogany table and grasped my hand. "I'm sorry, *macushla*. She was a lovely woman." I remembered then that he had danced with her at that Christmas party.

"And now, if you want to," he said, "you can tell me what you two are doing here, although I think I already know."

When I didn't answer, he said, "Why else should you be here except to try to find out who really killed that bastard? I never for a minute thought it was you, Sara."

I nodded. "But we never meant to involve you in it in any way. We didn't even mean for you to know we were here. So it will be best if you don't ask any questions."

He looked from me to Mike and then back again. "All right, no questions. But if you want to ask me any questions—"

After a moment, I said, "I guess I do. About the sanatorium. Is Swedenborg still running it?"

"Yes, and it's a bigger gold mine than ever, I hear."

I nodded. *People* magazine was one of the publications that circulated among Tattinger inmates. One issue, less than six months ago, had carried a story about Dr. Swedenborg and his patients who were rich or glamorous or famous or all three. As I'd read the article I had reflected that, evidently, Swedenborg's skill had come to outweigh his lack of charm.

What had made that issue of *People* especially popular with my fellow prisoners (although not with me) was it mentioned that Dr. Swedenborg's ex-partner had been the "handsome Dr. Covarrubias, slain by his lover, a young pianist whom the press dubbed 'the young Jean Harris.'"

Mike said, "We want to call Swedenborg."

After a moment Patrick Murray said, "Right away?"

Mike and I exchanged glances. "If possible," Mike said.

"Of course it's possible." Patrick Murray nodded toward a phone on a fine old Governor Winthrop desk across the room. "And since you want to leave me out of this, I'll get in some more of that walking the doc says is so good for me."

He went out. I saw him walk to the corner of the mansion and then strike out across what once must have been a beautiful lawn, toward a grove of willow trees.

As we had decided, I did the phoning. First a soft feminine voice said, "Serena Sanatorium. Good afternoon." Moments later a firmer one said, "Dr. Swedenborg's office."

"May I speak to Dr. Swedenborg, please?"

"I'm sorry. He's busy right now."

"Please tell him it's very, very important."

"Well, I'll try."

After perhaps a minute he said in an impatient voice, "Dr. Swedenborg."

"Do you recognize my voice, Doctor? Best not to use my name. But if you do recognize my voice, say so."

He waited several seconds and then said, "Yes." I was not surprised. True, it had been a long time since he had heard my voice. But like almost every TV listener and newspaper reader in the country, he must have known that I had escaped from Tattinger. And so it must have crossed his mind that I might show up here at Serena.

He said, "What do you want?"

"To talk to you."

"About what?"

"About something that happened in a field hospital near Hue, in Vietnam."

I heard his indrawn breath. He said, "I don't know what you're talking about."

"Yes you do." Then I tried the bluff Mike had suggested three nights ago in Los Cerritos. "I have a photocopy of a document concerning the incident."

After a moment's silence, he said, "I don't believe you."

216

But I could tell he did. The constriction of his voice told me that. And it convinced me, too, that it was he who had taken that document from Manuelo's safe. How often since then must he have awakened in the night, wondering if there were a copy someplace, wondering if it might surface when he least expected it to?

Fear had not robbed him entirely of his reasoning powers, though. He said, "If you had a copy, why didn't you use it earlier?"

He meant, why hadn't I used it at my trial, used it to show his good reason for wishing Manuelo Covarrubias dead.

Mike and I had prepared for that. "I didn't have it then," I said. "You'd better see me, Dr. Swedenborg."

He was silent for so long that I began to think something had gone wrong with the phone. Then he said, "Where?"

I had won the first skirmish.

"Do you know that little pond about two miles north of where the sanatorium's private road joins the highway?"

"Of course."

"Drive about two hundred yards beyond that. You'll see a track leading off to your right. If you follow it for about half a mile you'll come to a grove of live oaks. We'll be waiting tomorrow morning."

"We?"

"I have a friend. And Dr. Swedenborg?"

"Yes?"

"If you're thinking of sending the authorities instead of coming yourself, reconsider. You could still lose everything you've got. On the other hand, if you do as I ask, nothing will happen to you."

Unless, I added mentally, it was you who drove that knife into Manuelo's back.

"Tomorrow morning at ten?"

"Yes."

"Thank you, Dr. Swedenborg." I hung up.

"So he'll be there," Mike said.

"Yes, unless he decides to call the police instead."

"He won't. The guy's yellow. He proved that when he deserted his unconscious patient and scuttled into the bush. He'll be too afraid to go to the police, afraid to lose his sanatorium and his medical license. Maybe even afraid of landing in a military prison as a deserter. He'll figure his best bet, maybe his only bet, is to play ball with you."

He looked past me out the window. I turned to follow his gaze. With ostentatious slowness, Patrick Murray was approaching the carriage house.

We went outside, thanked him and said good-bye, and drove back to the little grove of live oaks.

21

Standing beside the RV the next morning, Mike and I watched a shiny black Bentley thread its way through the live oaks. The car stopped, and Carl Swedenborg got out. His tall figure and his thin face with its peevish mouth looked much the same. But his grayish-blue eyes were no longer merely discontented. They held acute anxiety.

I could tell that he was taking in the details of my own altered appearance, although he made no comment.

I said, "Dr. Swedenborg, this is Mike Rolfe." Neither man put out his hand. "Shall we go inside?"

When we entered the RV he looked with perceptible distaste at the scarred fold-down table and the worn leather seats. We sat down at the table, Mike and I on one side, Swedenborg on the other.

He said, "What proof can you give me

that you have such a document?" So, he had been thinking as well as worrying.

"I can tell you what's in it. You and Manuelo and some enlisted corpsmen were in a field hospital when an enemy barrage—"

He cut me off. "How did you get it?"

I launched into the fabrication Mike and I had worked out. "Manuelo gave it to me while I was nursing him through the flu. He came down with it soon after that Christmas I was here, remember?"

He gave a curt nod.

"It was in a sealed manila envelope he took from a drawer of the stand beside his bed. He told me that it was a copy of a document in his safe, and that he wanted me to take it to his lawyer in Milano, just in case something happened to the original. There was no urgency about it, he said. I could take it with me the next time I went shopping in Milano."

I paused. "You're the one who took the original document from the safe, aren't you? When did you do it? Before or after his murder?"

Sheer hatred showed in his eyes now. But when he spoke his voice was controlled. "After. One of the nurses had led you away. The police hadn't arrived yet. I ordered everyone out of the room, then opened the safe and found that statement of his. Of course I knew he'd made out such an affidavit. He'd held it over me for years."

"But the combination. How did you know how to open—"

"An afternoon about two weeks before, while I was standing out on that little balcony, Manuelo opened the safe for some reason. I guess he didn't realize that I could hear and memorize the clicks. Like nearly everyone, he made a brief pause before reversing the dial from right to left or vice-versa. So I didn't have much trouble that night getting the safe open.

"But we're not talking about that document," he went on. "We're talking about the copy you say you have."

"After Manuelo gave it to me, I took it to my room and put it in the lid pocket of my suitcase and then just forgot about it. After all, I had a lot on my mind." So much at least was true. I thought of that younger Sara, filled with terror at the thought of losing the most wonderful man in the world.

"After Manuelo got over the flu, I made a brief visit to my mother." Would Swedenborg remember, if he had ever known, that I had *not* paid such a visit? Mike and I had decided he would have had no reason to remember. "When I unpacked my suitcase at my mother's place, I saw there was a small tear in the lid pocket. I took everything out of the pocket and mended the tear. Then I forgot to put the envelope back. I just left it there, in the bureau in my old room. I— I guess it was what you could call Freudian forgetting."

He looked faintly surprised at my having known such a term. Then he gave a wintry smile. "I assume you mean that you were subconsciously trying to get back at him in little ways, such as ignoring his instructions."

"Yes. Anyway, I left it there. And shortly after I came back to Serena, I walked into Manuelo's apartment that night and found—"

I broke off, and then said, "I didn't once think of that envelope all through my trial or for weeks after they sent me to prison. Then my mother on one of her visits mentioned that she had found a sealed envelope in my old bureau. I got to thinking. One thing you do a lot of in prison, Dr. Swedenborg, is think." That, too, was true. "Maybe there was something in that envelope that would help explain what had happened to me. I didn't want her to mail it. The prison censor would have read it. So I asked her to open it and read it and then tell me on her next visit what it was about."

Again I paused. He asked, in a strained voice, "Well?"

"She did. I realized that the photocopy couldn't help me. Oh, it showed that you might have had your own reasons for killing Manuelo. But so might a number of other people. That document wouldn't help get me a new trial, not when I still had all that evidence against me—motive, opportunity, and those fingerprints. I realized I'd have to go on just as I had intended to, making the best of things, and trying not to add a single day to my sentence."

"But you broke out!"

"Yes. My—" I had been about to speak of my mother, but I didn't want to, not with this man, not unless I had to. "Yes, but something happened that forced me to. And now that I have, I've found every reason in the world—"

I looked at Mike, and we exchanged brief, taut smiles. "Now I need very much to remain free. And that's where you come in."

He just looked at me, his lips tight and a nerve jumping along his jawline.

I said, "Last night we went to my mother's house." Would he doubt that? Or would he think it probable that the police had given up watching for me there? "We have the document. It's in a different place now. A safe one. We won't use it if you'll do as we ask."

He didn't speak his question; he just looked at me.

"We have to find out what really happened in that sanatorium. And our only hope of doing that is to be inside for a while. We want you to get us in without anyone knowing who we are. Mike can be an orderly. I'll be a patient."

"A patient! Without anyone knowing who you are? You must be crazy. Plenty of people who knew you are still there. Domestic staff, medical staff. I'm not sure, but probably there are repeats among the patients—I mean, women who were there four years ago and have now come back. If you think that a different hair color and—"

Mike said, "Other people won't see her face."

Swedenborg's perceptions were quick. I could see that he had grasped the idea even before Mike explained it. "There must be medical procedures that involve bandaging the entire head and face. A complete face-lift, say, plus a nose operation—"

Tensely, Swedenborg nodded.

"I want to stay on the third floor," I said. "In my old room, if possible. Is it vacant?"

"It has been for months."

"Manuelo told me that V.I.P.'s occupied that room. Royalty and such. That is what I will be, some important person who has demanded that her identity be known to no one but yourself. A person who wants to be under your personal care, and who refuses to stay with the other patients on the second floor, even in a private room. Surely you can manage that."

He looked at me with bitter eyes.

Mike said, "You'd best cooperate, Doctor. And you'd best make sure we're safe there. If anything happens to us, the person with whom we left that photocopy will go to the police."

Swedenborg's voice sounded as if he were forcing the words out through an almost closed throat. "All right," he said. "All right."

22

Mid-afternoon two days later, I stood at the center of my old room at Serena, that third-floor room where I had felt so many emotions, ranging from the dreamy bliss of my first real love to the numb despair of an animal caught in a trap beyond its understanding.

Except for a few additions, the room looked the same. A new coverlet of a darker shade of blue on the bed. A mahogany-framed pier glass standing near that handsome old armoire. A white wicker magazine holder beside the bed.

In the pier glass I could see my reflection, rendered grotesque by the bandages that swathed my head, face, and neck, with openings only for my mouth and eyes—blue eyes, now. I had had the lenses nearly a month and they were beginning to irritate my eyes, when Mike had agreed—to my relief—that they wouldn't be necessary, not with the rest of my face hidden under gauze.

In the RV about an hour earlier Carl Swedenborg, fingers deft but eyes filled with helpless resentment, had applied a thin film of ointment to my face and then swiftly wound the bandages. The ointment, he had explained, was to keep the gauze from irritating my skin.

While he worked he told us in a grudging voice that, in accordance with our instructions, he had prepared the way for us at the sanatorium. Mike was to be a new orderly on the second floor, mopping halls and performing whatever other routine tasks were assigned to him by his immediate superior, a Puerto Rican named Renaldo Reyes. As for me, Swedenborg had told his staff that a very special patient was about to arrive, one who would stay on the third floor rather than in the sanatorium itself, and who would receive medical attention solely from him. He also mentioned the matter to two of his patients, which meant that by now every woman in the place knew that a strictly incognita V.I.P. was about to arrive.

In the sleek Bentley, the three of us drove to the sanatorium, Mike beside Dr. Swedenborg, I in the back. Mike got out of the car at the sanatorium's side entrance. Dr. Swedenborg drove around the corner of the building, then handed me out of the car. From the trunk he took the striped canvas suitcase that Mike and I had bought in Mil-

227

ano the day before. After all, I could hardly use the one I had bought in the Los Cerritos *barrio*.

As the doctor and I mounted the three steps to the building's entrance, I had a sickening memory of the day I had been led, under arrest, out this same door.

In silence we rode up in the little elevator. He opened the door for me, set my suitcase inside. "I forgot to ask," I said, "but I suppose you've taken over Manuelo's apartment on this floor." (I did not add, "Just as you took over full control of this highly profitable sanatorium.") But perhaps something in my tone told him I was thinking that, because two spots of color dyed his prominent cheekbones.

"Yes," he said. "I use it on the occasional nights when I stay over. Most nights, of course, I drive home to my wife and family."

I remembered then that Manuelo had said he had a wife and three children "down the valley."

"I'll be back later," he said, and left me.

Now I moved to the front window. Although sunny, the day was cool. Only three women, all in sweaters and dark pants, were stretched out on the chaises on the broad lawn. I went to the other window and looked below. Winter roses were in bloom, but still there was no water in the cement pool. Apparently the gardeners were waiting for settled warm weather before they filled the pool with water and tropical fish.

I turned, walked to the center of the room, and stood there, my gaze resting absently on my reflection in the pier glass. Were Mike and I just making fools of ourselves? After all, four years had passed since Manuelo's murder. The person responsible might be thousands of miles from here. He or she might be dead.

My eyes again swept the room. The pier glass, the old armoire, the little fireplace with its white marble mantel, the dressing table, the small writing desk, the bed . . .

Suddenly I felt it, a conviction that the person I sought *was* still here, beneath this roof. It was as if my slow survey of the room had aroused some sleeping memory, a memory that, if I could recapture it, would point me in the right direction.

Eagerly now, I again looked around the room. But this time I had no sense of something stirring just below the surface of my consciousness. Something *had* stirred, though. It was still down there, waiting for me to capture it.

I lifted my new suitcase onto the bed. Mike and I had decided it was exactly the sort of suitcase an important *incognita* might have chosen for the present purpose, luggage of good quality but not really expensive. After all, it was to be assumed that this case was just a temporary substitute for the lady V.I.P.'s usual luggage, opulent cases that bore her initials or even a ducal crest.

As for my clothes, thank God this was California, where even the richest women regard casual turtlenecks and pants as *de rigueur* for daytime, just as long as they are not made of—horrors!—polyester.

I began to take out my few belongings and place them in the bureau drawers and the closet.

23

About a quarter of an hour later I descended in the elevator to the wide ground-floor hall. As I passed the salon, I slowed my steps to look inside. No cocktail-drinking patients had assembled, but there were two people sitting on a chintz-covered sofa near the doorway. With a leap of my pulse, I recognized the woman. She was Elisa Dalton, the TV star with the almost pathologically jealous young husband. And the man with her now? Probably the husband. I couldn't be sure. If it was he, he wore much shorter hair now; and a bandage concealed his nose.

I wondered what sort of cocktail-hour entertainment was offered in the salon these days. (Later I was to learn the answer: none. The dour Dr. Swedenborg believed that expert medical care was enough without such frills as a cocktail pianist.) I went on out into the cool sunlight.

The three women were still stretched out on the lawn chairs. About a dozen feet from the group was another chair. As I walked toward it, the women broke off their conversation. I knew that it was not just my bandages that drew their attention. Several times during my months here four years ago I had seen women with bandaged heads and faces, lying in lawn chairs or walking the graveled paths. No, what interested them was the realization that I must be the mystery patient. I could almost hear their silent questions. Was I the wife of a Wall Street billionaire? A member of the British royal family? A rock star who had to shed fifteen years in order to appeal to a new generation of fans?

I nodded to the women, then stretched out on my chaise. After a moment one of the trio called, "Cool today, isn't it?"

"Yes."

I knew they must be mulling over that monosyllable. Had I sounded American? British? French?

I waited, knowing that they would not venture a personal question. (Although Serena was rife with gossip, the tacit code forbade specific questions about age, marital status, or even the exact nature of the treatment one was receiving. To learn such information, you had to find some third person who knew the answers.) I closed my eyes.

Another of the women tried. "You should have been here last week. The weather was like June."

"How nice." My heartbeat quickened. I had heard that voice before. I opened my eyes. Yes, and I had seen that face, the whole upper half of it masked by black glasses.

My first night here at Serena. Reflections of candlelight in the glass walls of the little balcony. Manuelo across the table from me, and bliss in my heart. Then that woman walking in, making her bitter accusation, whipping off the glasses to reveal her ruined face.

What was her name? It came to me. Winship, Paula Winship.

What was she doing back here?

The third woman tried. "Will you be having a cocktail in the salon?"

"No," I said, trying to sound politely regretful. "No cocktail."

I knew they must be wanting to ask if my refusal was based on medical or moral considerations. But that, of course, would be violating the unwritten code. Baffled, they fell silent.

I wanted to get up immediately and go to my room. Dr. Swedenborg had said he would be up to see me "later," and I did not want to risk missing him. Now I had questions to ask about Paula Winship and about that couple in the salon.

But it would seem odd to depart less than five minutes after I had arrived, and so I lay there with eyes closed for about a quarter of an hour, aware that although the women had resumed their talk they still must be scrutinizing me. Then I stood up, nodded a polite farewell, and went up the graveled walk and into the building.

I saw a few more people in the salon now. Elisa Dalton and the man with the bandaged nose were still there. Evidently some sort of quarrel had flared. Twenty minutes ago they had been sitting thigh-to-thigh. Now they sat well apart, both staring straight ahead. I hurried on to the elevator and up to my room.

Shadows were beginning to fill the room by the time I heard a light tap and then Dr. Swedenborg's voice. I let him in? and he said, without preamble, "Didn't you say that you want to take all your meals in your room?"

"Yes." I was afraid that if I were with people for too long at one time, some word or gesture might betray me. Besides, I knew that my bandaged face, plus the story Dr. Swedenborg had circulated about me, would make me the object of all eyes, something not conducive to enjoying one's food.

"Eunice Newcome, the girl who used to serve dinner to you and—and Manuelo—is no longer here." As before, he had a little trouble saying Manuelo's name. "She got married. I'll see that your dinner is served by a new girl—Irene. She serves my dinner whenever I stay here overnight.

"But as for your breakfast," he went on, "it will be served by Amy."

Amy, the pretty, giggly girl with the freckles and the red-gold hair done in two looped pigtails at the sides of her head.

"I could ask Mrs. Guerrero to assign someone else to bring your breakfast, but that would cause talk and—well, general upset."

I felt a fleeting sympathy for him. How he must be hoping that everything would be resolved with a minimum of "upset," leaving him still in possession of his freedom, his medical license, and his flourishing sanatorium.

"If I say as little as possible, there's not much chance Amy will recognize my voice." Then I suddenly remembered something he had said only a moment ago. "Mrs. Guerrero is still here?"

"Yes, she's still housekeeper. You thought I'd probably dismissed her?"

"Yes."

"Because she'd been part of my predecessor's life since he was a small child? That didn't alter the fact that she is competent at her job, and that it would have taken months and months for someone else to master the position of housekeeper in a place like this. Practical consideration dictated that I ask her to stay on."

I gave him grudging good marks for honesty. Another person might have said he had kept her on because at her age it would have been hard for her to find another job. He had given practicality as his reason. But then, cowards were practical people. The very vocabulary of cowardice—don't stick your neck out; better a live coward than a dead hero—all of that was eminently practical.

"I wouldn't be surprised," he went on, "if she pays you a call very soon. She's curious about you, and a little miffed with me for not telling her who my patient is. But I don't think she'll recognize your voice. She's a bit deaf, you know."

I hadn't realized it four years earlier. But looking back I recalled that sometimes she had failed to answer when I spoke to her. At the time I had assumed it was because of an inherent surliness, or disapproval of my affair with a man she thought of almost as a son. But now I realized that she might have been just hard of hearing.

"Well, I guess that's all," he said, and started to turn toward the door.

"Wait! I want to ask you about Elisa Dalton and her husband."

"Keith Chardine."

"Yes. I'd forgotten his name. I think I

saw him with her in the salon. Why is she here again?"

"She isn't here again, not as a patient. She's just staying here to keep her husband company. *He's* the patient. A nose job."

"Nose job!" I had thought him too handsome to require any sort of cosmetic surgery.

"He wants his nose to be straight rather than slightly aquiline." He gave one of his rare, icy smiles. "All foolishness of course, but I think he's still afraid of losing his wife. In show-biz parlance, she's hotter than ever now, you know."

I nodded. Not long after her role had been written out of the prime-time soap opera that had made her famous, another producer had hit upon the idea of a new kind of series, mixing the supernatural with the usual combination of sex, money, and skullduggery. The result was "Mansion on the Hill," which had made its star, Elisa Dalton, more famous than ever.

I said, "I saw Paula Winship, too."

He looked surprised. "You knew her? Why, she left here at least a couple of years before you came to Serena."

"She came back one night. Just walked into Manuelo's apartment and began to rail at him. Then she whipped off her glasses. It was all . . . very unpleasant."

He nodded. "But she's going to be all right." Pride in his voice. "I've managed to repair most of what Manuelo and that coked-up hack did to her."

I almost said, "It wasn't Manuelo's fault that she walked out of here before she had healed properly." I checked myself. What did it matter to anyone but Paula Winship now? Besides, considering the way Manuelo had managed to make me believe that we would spend the rest of our lives together, how could I be sure that he had told me the truth about Paula Winship or anything else?

"If there's anything more you'd like to ask—" That little flare of pride had left his voice and he once more sounded nervous and depressed.

"There isn't."

"Then I'll look in on you sometime tomorrow." My gaze must have held a question, because he said in an irritated voice, "You are supposed to be my patient, remember, under my personal medical care. That means I'll have to spend some time in your room, ostensible to check the progress of your healing."

He left then. Almost an hour later someone knocked. When I called, "Who is it?" a timid little voice said, "It's Irene, with your dinner."

Obviously, Swedenborg had not subscribed to Manuelo's theory that an establishment such as this one should have an attractive staff. Irene was indisputably plain. Not ugly, just plain, and in every way too thin—thin face framed by thin hair of an indefinite brown-blond shade; long, thin nose; thin lips over rabbity teeth. There was a rabbit-like timidity about her, too.

Perhaps she had not yet become inured to the sight of gauze-wrapped heads and faces. I could almost hear her wondering if it was Princess Margaret under the bandages.

She said, "Ma'am, where—"

I gestured toward the small table standing beside the front window. With a nervous clatter, she set the tray down, said she hoped I would enjoy my dinner, and scuttled to the door. I settled down to braised sirloin tips and asparagus. When I had finished, I put the tray out in the hall. In a little while I heard the rattle of silver against china and knew that Irene was picking the tray up.

At ten I was already in bed, reading a copy of *The New Yorker* from the magazine rack beside me, when someone tapped lightly on the door: two taps, a pause, two more taps, and a final tap. It was the signal Mike and I had agreed upon. I tossed the magazine aside, picked up my robe from a chairback, and hurriedly put it on over my nightgown. I opened the door, and he slipped inside the room and put his arms around me. We held each other tight. Then I said, "Let me look at you."

Mike would have made a most unlikely-looking orderly, even in a uniform that fitted. This one did not. The white blouse was too short, especially in the sleeves, and his pants ended a couple of inches above his bony ankles.

"Oh, Mike!" I said.

"Don't laugh. You look pretty weird yourself, you know."

"I know. How's the job?"

"Terrible. Remind me to never take up this kind of work. But enough of that." He reached under his blouse and took a gun from inside the waistband of those too-short pants. "Keep this in the drawer right beside your bed."

I shook my head. "I've never even touched a pistol in my whole life."

"It's not a pistol. It's a revolver. And it's loaded, but as long as you keep the safety on—that's this little gizmo right here—it can't go off. If you want to fire, push the safety off, like so, and pull the trigger." He put the safety back on.

"Mike! I don't want it."

"Yes you do."

"I don't! And where did you get it?"

"From the head orderly. He had it in his car."

"Why?"

"Why did he have it? I didn't ask him."

"What did you say about why you wanted it?"

"He didn't ask me. But I told him I planned to do some target shooting in the hills." He walked to my bedside stand, opened the little drawer, and put the gun inside. "Now keep it there."

He walked back to me. I said nothing. Much as I hated the idea of handling that gun, its presence made me feel a little safer.

"Have you seen where you'll sleep?" I asked.

"Yes. It's not bad. Two guys to a room, and the beds look comfortable."

He put his arms around me. "Speaking of which," he said, and I realized he was looking over my shoulder at my bed. "Even though you're done up in all that gauze, I still find you—"

"No, Mike." Not that I didn't want him. In spite of that notebook—was he still writing in it? I wondered—he could stir desire in me. I went on, "We can't risk your slipping out of here in the middle of the night. I'm not the only one on this floor, you know." Dr. Swedenborg had said he was staying overnight. Mrs. Guerrero's room was on this floor. Elisa Dalton almost certainly was occupying a room up here while her husband had his handsome face remodeled on the floor below. There might be even more occupants of the rooms along this corridor.

"If anyone sees you leaving now, they'll think Dr. Swedenborg sent an orderly up here for one reason or another. But if you're seen slipping from this room later on . . ."

He said, after a moment, "You're right, of course." Despite the gauze, he managed to find my lips. Then he slipped out into the hall, and I closed the door behind him.

24

A light tapping on my door woke me to hazy sunlight. Amy came in, bearing a breakfast tray. She looked scarcely a day older than when I last had seen her. Her pert face, with its upturned nose, was still so pretty that her freckles seemed a charming decoration rather than any sort of blemish.

"Good morning, ma'am," she said, avid curiosity in her bright blue eyes. Well, I had expected that. What I had not expected was the nervousness in her manner. Except for that morning after Manuelo's death, when she had been—or at least appeared to be—somewhat afraid of me, she had never impressed me as the nervous type.

"Where shall I put the tray?"

I indicated the bedside table. As she placed the tray there, I again experienced the stir of buried memory: something about Amy, and a tray of food on that table. I could not identify it, and yet I had a strong feeling that it was somehow related to Manuelo's death.

"Will you require anything else, ma'am?"

Require. I had never known Amy to speak

with such elegance. But then, she could not be sure she was not addressing royalty.

My reply also was unwontedly elegant. "Thank you. It is sufficient." Since I am no good at assuming other accents, I had decided that my best course with Amy would be to speak in a stilted manner.

She went out. I ate most of my excellent breakfast—orange juice, scrambled eggs, and toast—and placed the tray out in the hall. I had just finished dressing when someone knocked and said, "It is the housekeeper."

Hastily I stretched out on the chaise longue. "Please enter."

She came in. I saw that she had aged a lot in four years. Her hair was almost entirely gray now, and the lines bracketing her wide, firm-lipped mouth had deepened. But her figure still appeared strong and erect, and the carriage of her head dignified.

"My name is Mrs. Guerrero," she said. "I came to ask if you are comfortable."

I nodded, and then said, "Quite comfortable, thank you."

To test her hearing, I had spoken in a very soft voice. Her faint frown told me that she had been unable to hear me. She had understood the nod, though.

She said, "I am glad." She looked around her. "This is a very nice room."

"Very nice."

"It was mine when the sanatorium first opened."

I almost said, "Yes, I know." I checked myself, appalled, and then said, "So?"

"Yes. Later I decided that it would be more convenient for me to be near the service stairs, in case the elevator broke down. It did that sometimes in the early days, right after Dr. Covarrubias started the sanatorium."

She paused, and then said, "He was killed. Murdered." Her bleak, dark eyes looked directly into mine. With a rippling chill, I wondered what she would say or do if she realized she was in the same room with the young woman who had been sent to prison for that murder.

"But I suppose you know about that," she added.

I hesitated, then shook my head.

"You don't? I thought everyone in this country—But then, perhaps in Europe—"

It was an obvious invitation for me to say something about my origins. I said nothing at all. Finally she turned toward the door.

"If there is anything you want, madam, please let me know."

About a half hour after she had left me I took the elevator down to the ground floor and then walked along the broad hall to the front terrace. That faint haze was gone, and pleasantly warm sunlight poured down on the velvety grass and the groups of women in lawn chairs. A rapid survey indicated that neither Paula Winship nor Elisa Dalton was among them. Perhaps they had gone to Milano, or were in their rooms, or in some corner of the salon invisible to me as I'd passed its wide doorway.

There was an empty chaise near the foot of the stairs leading from the terrace to the lawn. Seated there, I would be in earshot of a group of five women, but far enough away to discourage any idea they might have of including me in their conversation. The group fell silent as I came down the steps, walked to the empty chaise, and stretched out. There was an appreciable interval before they resumed their talk—something about a woman named Maude who had tried to sue the government after the Coast Guard had searched her yacht for drugs. Eyes closed, I listened.

After a while I heard an engine's smooth

purr. I opened my eyes to see a black Porsche coming up the drive. Its driver was a red-haired young man. The girl beside him was brunette.

The car stopped and the girl got out. Nerves tightening, I saw that she was Gabriella Montgomery, as beautiful as ever—perhaps even more so. Gabriella of the sad gray eyes, who had taken my place in Manuelo's affections if not in his bed. He hadn't had time for that.

She would have succumbed to him, though. That day in Milano, when I saw her lunching with him, she obviously had been as helplessly in love as I was. What had she felt when she heard of his violent death? It may sound strange, but it was the first time I had asked myself that question. All during my arrest and trial, my incarceration in Tattinger and my escape from it, I had been too taken up by the enormity of what was happening to me to give much thought to that other girl.

Whatever pain Manuelo's death had brought her, she was in love with someone else now. It showed in her face as she leaned across the door of the low-slung car to make some laughing remark to the red-haired young man. She turned and started up the steps.

"Fifteen minutes, remember!" he called after her. He was handsome indeed, I saw now, with a straight, short nose and an athlete's square jaw. And he was of her own generation. "If you're not out here when I get back, I'll drive away without you."

The smile she threw him over her shoulder said that his was an empty threat. Obviously he adored her. He drove on around the U-shaped drive and headed back toward the pillared entrance.

I heard one of the women say something about "the Montgomery girl."

"Who's the boy?"

"Charlie Pope. They're engaged, you know."

"I knew she was engaged to someone named Pope. I just didn't know what he looked like, that's all."

"A hunk, a beautiful hunk."

"That he certainly is."

A woman with a Deep South accent said, "I met her just once, about three years ago. She looked so tragic, especially for a girl that young."

"You don't know about her? She grew up with that look. Her mother died when she

248

was ten or so. Then, when she was twelve, her father, whom she absolutely adored, shot himself. Some say he was manic-depressive. Anyway, she walked into his den and found the body."

"Oh, the poor little thing."

A voice I hadn't heard before spoke. "They say she and Manuelo Covarrubias had something going, just before that Hargreaves girl killed him."

Absurd to feel anger, but I found my fist clenching.

"I don't believe it," someone else said. "In spite of her father's suicide, the Montgomerys have always been considered top-drawer. She wouldn't have had anything to do with a notorious tomcat like Manuelo Covarrubias. Besides, she couldn't have been more than eighteen then, and he was more than twice that."

"All the more reason, if she was so devoted to her father. You see, she was looking for someone to take his place—"

"Oh, Nancy! You and your amateur psychology."

Silence for perhaps a minute. Then someone asked the question that had been on my mind.

"Why is she here today?"

"Certainly not for a face-lift! Does anyone know?"

No one spoke.

After a few seconds someone said something more about the woman whose yacht had been raided. I tuned their conversation out, and went on thinking about Gabriella. That day in Milano when, in jealous torment, I had looked at her lunching with Manuelo, I wondered where I had seen her before. Now, four years later, I suddenly remembered.

It had been right here, at Serena, on Christmas Day, that wonderful Christmas when I had been so happy. It was the one day of the year, Manuelo said, when everyone was invited to Serena—the entire neighborhood, the sanatorium staff and patients, and any of their relatives who cared to come. There had been a cacophony—Patrick Murray's bagpipes, laughter, shouts, the pounding rhythms of the country-western band. And somewhere in all that crush I'd had a glimpse of Gabriella Montgomery. Had she been dancing? Yes, that was it. With Patrick Murray, of all people, she had been two-stepping to "The Yellow Rose of Texas."

Was that the first time Manuelo had seen her? Perhaps. Perhaps on that day, which had seemed to me so blissful, the whole tragic course of events had been set in motion.

I glanced at my watch. Surely Gabriella had been in there almost fifteen minutes. She would be coming out soon. Turning my head, I fixed my gaze on the sanatorium entrance.

Gabriella appeared at the top of the steps and came down. Just as she reached the graveled drive, I called, "Miss Montgomery!"

She halted, giving me a startled look. Then, with a polite, puzzled smile she walked over to stand beside my chair.

"Forgive me for speaking to you," I said, in a voice low enough to defeat the (no-doubt) straining ears of those five women. "But I recognized you from your picture in the papers." That was safe enough to say. An engaged member of a "top-drawer" San Jose family would of course have had her engagement photo in the paper. "Such a lovely picture. Anyway, I wanted to wish you happiness."

"Thank you, ma'am," she said, hesitating a little. Plainly, in spite of those obscuring bandages, she had sensed I was not much older than herself.

"My name is Wilson, Joan Wilson. Mrs."

"How do you do, Mrs. Wilson."

"Tell me," I said in a playful tone, "you're not having a face-lift, are you?"

She smiled. "I came here to see my aunt."

"Oh? And who is your aunt?"

"Well, she isn't exactly my aunt. Sort of an honorary aunt. You know how it is if while you're growing up there's an older person close to your family—"

She broke off. The black Porsche had driven through the sanatorium entrance. "Oh, excuse me, Mrs. Wilson, but I'll have to go." I could understand the relief in her voice. It must be disconcerting to talk to a person whose face you can't see. "Nice to have met you."

She hurried down the drive. The Porsche stopped and she got in. She waved as the car drove past me and then circled around to head back toward the entrance.

I threw a swift look at the group of women. It was plain from their baffled expressions that they had gleaned even less than I had from my few moments with Gabriella Montgomery. I waited a little while, then got up and went into the building.

Amy brought me my lunch. She exhibited less of that blend of curiosity and nervousness I had seen in her manner that morning.

252

Perhaps she was just controlling it better. When I had finished eating I put the tray out in the hall and then sat at the dressing table, filing my nails.

Soon after I heard Amy take the tray away, someone knocked. Even before he announced himself, I was sure it was Dr. Swedenborg.

He came in, carrying a copy of the *Journal of the American Medical Association* in his left hand, with his forefinger marking his place. "Just go on with what you're doing," he said in an irritated voice. He sat down beside the window. "I'll read for fifteen minutes and then leave."

"I need the answers to some questions, Doctor."

He looked up from the *Journal*. "Well?"

"Do you know a Gabriella Montgomery?" When he merely frowned at me, I said, "Manuelo was in love with her just before —I mean, there at the last."

"I never even tried to keep track of Manuelo's—" Whatever he was about to say, he decided against it. "No, I don't know anyone of that name."

"She was here today. Perhaps you saw her. She's a very beautiful girl—"

"My dear young woman! Besides yourself,

253

the only women I've seen today received an abdominal liposectomy and a chin augmentation. Neither of them looked beautiful, especially not on the operating table!"

He sounded angry. But I knew that in the main it was false anger. What he felt most keenly was fear.

"She must have been visiting one of your patients, some sort of relative. At least Gabriella calls her aunt—"

"God damnit! Except for a twenty-minute lunch break, I've been in the operating theater since this morning. Do you think I have time to check up on who has a niece visiting her? Now let me read!"

He read, or at least pretended to. I finished my nails and then just stared out the window. Finally he must have decided he had stayed long enough to convince any chance observer that he had been ministering to my medical needs. He stood up, said, "Good day," and left.

25

When he had gone I wandered restlessly about the room, fiddling with objects on my dressing table and on the little desk, opening the desk drawer to look at the stack of letter paper and the neatly aligned ballpoint pens. I was turning over in my mind my conversations with Gabriella and Dr. Swedenborg and Mrs. Guerrero and even Amy.

Suddenly I wondered about Amy and Manuelo. Had he never been drawn to that unusual freckled prettiness of hers? And had she never regarded the handsome and famous Dr. Covarrubias as anyone but her employer? Probably I could never know the answer to that question.

I went over to the bedside magazine holder and reached down for *The New Yorker* I had been reading. It was not until then that I realized I had picked up the letter opener from the desk and still held it in my hand. I walked back to the desk, laid the letter opener on the blotter, and turned around. Then I stood stock still.

There could be no doubt that my fingerprints were on the broad silver handle of the letter opener, just as they had been on the ivory handle of that knife that killed Manuelo. And yet, lost in thought, I'd had no more memory of picking up the letter opener than I'd had of picking up that African hunting knife.

But wait. There was a big difference. Anyone might absently pick up a loose object like that letter opener and carry it about for a few minutes. But to make those prints on the hunting-knife handle I would have had to open that glass-topped case and pick up one of those weapons I had regarded with such distaste the moment I saw them. *That* I could not have done absent-mindedly. That I would have remembered doing.

I went back to the magazine rack.

Soon after dark Irene arrived with my dinner tray. Looking almost as timid as the night before, she put the tray on the table beside the window and then left.

The one-dish meal, an individual tureen of oyster chowder, was excellent. I savored not only the oysters and cream and potatoes, but even the finely minced onion and carrots and celery. When I had finished the last drop I put the tray out in the hall. Then I resumed my reading, this time from an issue of *West Coast Magazine*.

In the distance there was a mutter of thunder. The window curtain billowed inward on a cooling breeze. It was going to rain, but whether it would be a passing shower or one of those three-day California downpours, only time would tell.

Around eight Mike came to my room. I

told him of Gabriella's visit and asked if he knew whom she had come to see.

"No use asking me, darling. Carlos had me wrestling crates of newly arrived equipment down in the basement all day. New guy always gets the dirty work, you know. But I'll ask the other orderlies and let you know what they say. You want me to do that right now?"

"No, I don't think so." For the last few minutes I had been feeling tired, surprisingly so for that hour. "But if you could slip up here tomorrow as soon as you learn anything—"

"That I will." Again he managed to find my lips despite all that gauze. We held each other tight for a moment. Then he left. I undressed, fell into bed, and slept.

And dreamed.

I dreamed that someone was in my room, someone who had brought with him weird noises—drum rolls and cymbal-like clangs. And he was doing something very strange, bathing my face in cool water. Then the noises lessened, ceased, and the dream ended, or perhaps merged with a different one. I can't be sure.

When I awoke I stared in befuddlement at the changing light that came through the window curtains. Watery sunlight would give way to grayness, then to pale sunlight again. After a moment I realized that this must be the final stage in the breakup of a nighttime storm: low clouds were revealing, then concealing, weak sunlight that filtered through a high overcast.

The rain must have been heavy; the window curtains hung in sodden folds. The polished bare boards beneath the windows were wet. Warned by the distant growl of thunder, I should have closed the windows last night, no matter how tired I felt.

I glanced at my watch. Not quite eight. With guilty haste I went into the bathroom, seized a heavy bath towel, and returned to the windows. I sopped up the water from the floorboards, then straightened the folds in the curtains so they would dry more quickly. I still felt tired. What was more, my head ached dully.

I took the wet towel into the bathroom and dropped it into the tub. As I started back into the bedroom, I remembered my dream. The rolling of drums and the crash of cymbals must have been evoked by thunder and by lightning bolts striking nearby. But why had I dreamed that someone was in this room, bathing my face with cool water?

Moisture-laden air blowing through an open window onto my face could have caused that part of the dream, I reasoned. No, that couldn't be. I wouldn't have felt damp coolness through those layers of gauze.

My hand flew to my face. The bandage felt different. Once taut and smooth, the outer layer was now slack along my cheeks, under my chin—

I whirled, looked at my reflection in the pier glass mirror. The bandages also looked different now.

Someone *had* been in this room during the night. Someone had removed that bandage, seen my face, and then rewound the gauze with fingers less expert than those of Dr. Swedenborg.

Someone who had only suspected I was Sara Hargreaves now knew it for sure.

My body tingled with fear. At the same time, I felt a certain triumph. I had been right. My enemy was here at Serena. An enemy who had killed Manuelo Covarrubias after trying to make sure that I would be the one to pay for the murder. Made desperate by fear, that person had drugged me into insensibility and then invaded this room.

It had been the oyster chowder, of course. All those rich flavors had masked a heavy dose of barbiturate or some other soporific. Drugs of almost any sort were easy to come by in a place like Serena.

But who had slipped that drug into the tureen? Impossible to believe that it could have been Irene—timid, homely Irene who had not even been here at the time of Manuelo's death. But Amy had been here—

I looked at my watch. Amy would be bringing my breakfast at any moment. I hurried to my bed.

About two minutes later there was a knock. "It's Amy, ma'am." I called to her to come in.

As she crossed the room, I kept my eyes fixed on her face. Was there anything different in her appearance or behavior this morning? I could not be sure. True, she had kept her own gaze fixed on the tray as she moved toward the bed, but that might have been because she feared that pretty little cream pitcher might spill over. Perhaps she had done the same thing the day before. Perhaps, once you begin to suspect a person, everything that person does seems odd, even sinister.

As on the day before, I gestured toward the bedside table and she put the tray down.

It was then that I recaptured one of the memories that had eluded me yesterday.

On the afternoon of that terrible day four years ago, I had entered this room to find a belated lunch—a ham sandwich and a glass of milk—awaiting me on that bedside table. I could recall just assuming that Amy had brought it. After all, she was the one assigned to various day-duties on the first and third floors. I had eaten the lunch and then, almost immediately, fallen asleep. When I awakened, feeling tired and heavy-limbed, much as I had felt upon awakening this morning, I had gone to Manuelo's apartment and found him there in the dimly lit room, stretched out face down on the Oriental rug. . . .

I was sure now that I had been drugged that afternoon four years ago. Oh, the dosage had not been as heavy as the one in last night's oyster chowder. But it had been heavy enough so that someone could enter this room, and fold my limp right hand around that knife's broad handle, so that it received the impress of my fingertips—

It could have happened like that. It *must* have happened like that. How else could my fingerprints have been found on an object which I had never touched or even thought of touching?

I looked from the breakfast tray up into Amy's eyes. In the instant before she veiled them with her red-gold lashes, I again saw avid curiosity there. But had there been a sly hint of triumph, too—the triumph of now knowing whose face was hidden by all that gauze?

She said, "Will there be anything else, ma'am?"

"Yes. Will you please take a message to Dr. Swedenborg? I would like to see him as soon as possible."

She looked startled, perhaps just by the idea of anyone issuing such a peremptory summons for the god-like chief of the Serena sanatorium.

"I'll try, ma'am."

"Please do."

"Enjoy your breakfast, ma'am."

When she had left me I turned my attention to the tray. It was a continental breakfast this morning—orange juice, flaky croissants with little pots of jam, plus coffee and cream. Should I eat it? No, I decided. Why take a chance? Besides, whatever had been put in that oyster dish had left me feeling a little queasy.

In the bathroom I disposed of all the food except the croissants. Those I took over to the window. I unhooked the screen, tore the croissants into small pieces, and placed them on the outer sill. Minutes after some sharp-eyed California jay spotted them, the last crumbs would be gone. I put the tray out into the hall, then got dressed and stretched out on the chaise longue to wait for Dr. Swedenborg.

I did not have to wait long. Less than five minutes later there was a knock on the door. I called out, "Who is it?" and when he gave his name I asked him to come in.

The resentment in his face was even more pronounced than usual. Plainly, he was outraged that I was able to summon him as I might the humblest of his employees. But when I told him what had happened, the peevishness in his face gave way to fear, almost to panic. Any faint suspicion I held that he himself was the one who had killed his partner vanished at that moment. The near-certain knowledge that the killer was still here at Serena was plainly as much of a shock to him as it had been to me.

He bent to look at my gauze-wrapped face. "Yes, those bandages were removed all right." He began to pace the floor.

After perhaps a minute he stopped before me and said, "I've been thinking. Suppose I give you and your young man fifty thousand dollars. You can go somewhere where you'll be safe. Central America, the Middle East, anyplace. You're both young and strong and intelligent. You'll be able to make your way anywhere."

I knew that it was not concern for my safety that prompted his offer. It was concern that another violent episode would ruin the reputation of his sanatorium. Even worse, a new investigation might bring to light that long-ago incident in Vietnam.

"All I'll want in return for the fifty thousand," he said, "is that—that photocopy you have."

His mention of that non-existent document brought me a twinge of guilt. But he would never have helped us to get into Serena if we had not held some sort of threat over him!

"Dr. Swedenborg, we promised you we would not make trouble for you if you would just cooperate with us."

He said, almost as if I hadn't spoken, "All right. I'll make it seventy-five thousand. But that's as high as I can go. I'm not rich. The sanatorium makes a lot, but I've got three children, two in college and one—"

I shook my head. I had no intention of living out my life as a fugitive, a fugitive guiltless of the crime for which I had been imprisoned.

He seemed about to explode. "Don't you realize that whoever drugged you and unwrapped those bandages could easily have killed you last night? Making sure of your identity was only the first step. Right now he—" He broke off. "You're sure you don't know whether it was a man or a woman?"

"No. I just had a sense of a presence beside the bed."

"Well, one thing you *can* be sure of. Right now the person who was here last night is trying to figure out the safest way of ridding himself of you."

"Yes, I know." I think I must have sounded much braver than I felt. The thought of my hidden enemy beneath this roof, an enemy who already had killed once, made my stomach knot up.

"But I won't go back to Tattinger. And I won't spend the rest of my life running because of a crime I didn't commit. And that means I have to find out who killed Manuelo. Don't *you* want to know?"

"Of course, but—" He stopped. I could imagine what he was thinking. As long as his sanatorium flourished, he could live with the thought of a hidden killer, a killer who probably would remain quiescent once my threatening presence was removed.

He said, "Perhaps you'll change your mind if you talk it over with your friend. Shall I send him up here?"

"Please do."

"Good-bye, then." He turned abruptly and left the room.

A few minutes later Mike tapped his signal on the door. I opened it and he walked in, his face so pale and worried that I knew Dr. Swedenborg had told him what had happened during the night. Nevertheless, he asked me to repeat the story, and I did. Then I said, "Did he mention the money?"

"What money?"

"He offered fifty thousand, and then seventy-five, if we'd just disappear."

"What did you say?"

"No, of course. I won't be a permanent fugitive myself, let alone turn you into one. And I'm not going to give you up."

He caught me close against him. "No, we won't run. And we'll think of the right thing to do. But in the meantime, I'll bring you all your meals, directly from the kitchen. When you're outside your room, stay with people. No walks by yourself. And when you're in your room, keep your door locked."

"But I don't have a key."

"Yes, you do. I think one of these should fit." He reached into the pocket of his white blouse and brought out four skeleton keys. "Just before I came up here I got these from a supply closet."

The second key he tried fitted the lock. "Now when you're inside this room, leave the key in the lock, so that no one else can insert a key."

I nodded, and then asked, "Have you found out anything about who it was that Gabriella Montgomery was visiting?"

"No, I've drawn a complete blank."

He put his hands on each side of my bandaged head and kissed my lips. I said, "All this gauze. After last night, it seems rather unnecessary to leave it on."

"Just the same, leave it be until we can think this whole thing through. I'll bring your lunch as near to one o'clock as I can."

Perhaps it was the protective tenderness in his voice. Perhaps it was the unnerving knowledge that my enemy was right here beneath this roof. Whatever the reason, I suddenly felt I could no longer bear the additional burden of my secret mistrust. I had to bring it into the open.

I said, "Mike, that notebook."

"What are you talking about?" No guilt in his face, just puzzlement.

"That notebook you've been keeping about me." My voice sounded thick. "I found it in your bookcase at the motel."

Still no guilt in his face, just surprise and concern. "When did you find it?"

"One of our last nights at the motel. You'd gone up to fix the bathtub plug in one of the rooms."

He nodded. "I remember."

"Why, Mike? Why have you been writing down all those things, without even mentioning it to me?"

"I didn't tell you because I didn't want you to know how worried I was. You see, when I began that notebook I felt sure that sooner or later you were going to be caught. I wouldn't be able to defend you in court. But maybe I could help whoever it was who eventually would defend you. If I could hand him a dossier that included every little fact about you that might help your case,

268

every detail that might make a judge and jury feel more sympathetic toward you—"

"Oh, Mike!" I felt shame flooding through me.

"What is this, Sara? Why didn't you ask me about those notes as soon as you found them?"

"I . . . I don't know." Someday I would tell him how I had suspected him of using me, exploiting me to make money and to further his career. But right now I was too ashamed. Right now all I wanted was to stand in his embrace for a few moments. I laid my cheek against his chest, and his arms went around me.

I asked in a muffled voice, "Are you still keeping notes?"

"Not these past few days. In fact, I left the notebook locked up in the RV back in that oak grove. I felt it would be too dangerous to bring it right into the sanatorium. Besides, I don't think now that you're going to need any high-powered defense. We're going to find the son of a bitch who did this to you, Sara. And when we do, you'll be in the clear, jail break or no jail break. You spent nearly four years in prison for something you didn't do. After that, no court is going to send you back to do more time. All we have to do right now is to keep you safe."

He tilted my face and kissed me again. "Now lock the door after me."

26

When Mike had gone, I tried to lock the door. His fingers had turned the key easily. Mine had difficulty. Perhaps the lock needed oiling, or perhaps the two halves of the lock were a little out of line. It was not until I pounded on the door with the heel of my other hand, just above the keyhole, that the key finally turned. Leaving the key in the lock, I stretched out on the chaise and tried, in Mike's phrase, "to think this whole thing through."

But the dream that had been no dream kept blocking my way. Someone had been in this room, a dark, looming presence beside my bed. Had he used some sort of light? He must have. Probably it had been a pencil flashlight, its glow dimmed and diffused by a handkerchief or some other cloth placed over the lens. The thought of him, slowly unwinding the gauze and then shining the dim light on my drugged, helpless features, seemed infinitely repugnant. Although the last of the storm clouds had passed and sunlight now lay warm in the room, I felt chilled.

I needed to get away from this room where it had happened, a room so silent that the tick of the mantel clock sounded loud.

Stay with the crowd, Mike had said. All right, I would.

I went to the door. Again the key resisted. Rattling the knob, banging on the door, I finally managed to turn it. Out in the hall, I had to go through the same noisy procedure before I was able to lock the door. Finally, though, the key turned.

I withdrew it, dropped it in my skirt pocket, and headed not for that often-slow elevator but for the front stairs. Before descending, though, I stopped at the long hall window and looked down at the lawn: lots of patients out there, under a sky polished to a bright blue by last night's storm. There were seven or eight women near the front steps. I would move a chair quite close to them, close enough that they would be sure to ask me to join their group.

For a few moments I studied the groups on the wide lawn. Elisa Dalton of the flaming hair was not among them, nor was her young husband. Neither was Paula Winship, with her black glasses obscuring a ruined face that, Dr. Swedenborg had said, would be much improved after his remedial surgery. Satisfied that I had surveyed everyone visible from this hall window, I turned toward the stairs.

I don't know whether or not, in the instant before I turned, I heard a sound several yards behind me in the hall. But I do think I heard the sibilance of the knife as it turned, end-over-end, through the air. I think I even felt, for a tiny fraction of a second, the rush of air as it passed. Then the blade lodged itself, handle still aquiver, in the frame of the long window. I don't think it would have struck me even if I hadn't moved, but it would have been close.

As I stared at the knife, I felt I could hear it vibrating. Then I realized it was just the seething of my own blood in my ears.

But now I did hear something, a subdued click, as if a door along the hall had closed very softly. I whirled around, peering into the dim hall stretching behind me. Nothing. No one.

After an instant I looked back at the embedded knife, feeling a strange mixture of terror and triumphant relief. Something, probably shock, now had brought that other buried memory to the surface of my mind.

I was almost sure who had killed my middle-aged lover. I was almost sure how it had been accomplished. What I did not yet know was *why*.

Then fear blotted out my sense of triumph. Fumbling for the key in my pocket, I ran to my door and inserted the key in the lock, throwing a glance along the hall. Still nothing, no one. *Again* the lock resisted. I could feel sweat on my face under the gauze before the key finally turned.

I went inside, closed the door, and forced the key to turn. I pulled the dressing table bench over to the armoire, climbed onto it, and reached far back onto the deep shelf. It was still there. My fingertips touched it. Stretching even farther, I grasped the roll of paper and stepped down from the bench. Hands shaking now, I unrolled the old circus poster, with its Human Cannonball tumbling across the upper half. My gaze dropped to the list of names under "also starring." They were third on the list: Juanito el Cuchillo and Constancia.

Like most Californians, I have a smattering of Spanish, enough to know that in English that third line read, "Johnny the Knife and Constancia."

A knife-throwing act, with "Constancia" as the target who stood against a tall cork board while Johnny outlined her body with flung steel blades.

Long ago, when I had first looked at this poster, on that happy day soon after I took possession of this room, I had paid no more attention to Juanito el Cuchillo's name than to any of the others. There had been no reason to. I had no idea then that a knife blade, lodged deep in his back, would destroy Manuelo's life and all but ruin mine.

I rolled up the poster, placed it on my dressing table, and hurried to the nightstand beside my bed. Too grim with determination now even to feel repugnance at the sight and feel of the gun Mike had given me, I thrust it deep into my pocket. I unlocked my door after a brief struggle, dropped the key into my other pocket, and went down the shadowy, silent hall. I didn't knock. I just touched the handle, and the door opened.

27

She sat on a rocker, hands folded in the lap of her dark skirt. The face she turned to me was so dull-eyed and hopeless in its frame of gray hair that I knew why she hadn't even bothered to lock her door. When that knife missed me, she knew that I, or someone, would be coming here soon.

I took the gun from my pocket and released the safety, just as Mike had showed me. The clicking sound was distinct in the stillness. I sat down on the edge of a straight chair about twelve feet from her.

"I'm very nervous," I said. "I've never handled a gun before. If you rush at me, or even move suddenly, I'm almost sure to fire."

Even as I spoke, my words sounded to me absurd. The woman in the rocker looked too weak and hopeless even to get up, let along rush me and try to wrest the gun from my grasp.

"You killed Manuelo, didn't you?" I said. "You held that knife by the tip and threw it so that it lodged between his shoulder blades."

After a long while she said in a dull voice, "Yes."

I felt a stir of rage. "That was how you kept from blurring my fingerprints, wasn't it?"

"Yes."

"You learned to throw knives when you were part of a circus act."

A touch of surprise brightened her dull gaze. "How did you know about the circus?"

"An old poster. It's been in that armoire in my room, probably for years and years. I saw it four years ago, but it wasn't until today that I connected it with you."

"That old poster," she said in that flat voice. "I thought I'd brought it with me when I moved into this room."

Her eyes wandered over the room. I too looked around for a quick moment or two, taking in the bed piled high with embroidered sofa pillows of clashing colors; the cheap reproduction of Gainsborough's "Pinkie" on one wall; framed photographs, too far away for me to see their subjects, on a small table against the wall opposite. I think I would have found it a depressing room even if I hadn't known who lived here.

She was looking at me now. I could see the memories gathering in her dark eyes.

276

Wistful memories, and angry ones, and tragic ones; memories that for too long had remained unspoken. I had a feeling that in a way she welcomed my forcing her to speak of them now.

"Is your real name Constancia?"

"One of my names. I was christened Maria Elena Constancia."

"And this Juanito? He was your husband?"

"No, I was only a young girl then." Leaning forward a little, she began to speak rapidly. They were bursting forth now, those dammed-up events I had seen in her eyes. "He was my uncle, the only family I had. My parents were both born in Guatemala— they were killed when I was twelve. They had a highwire bicycle act, with my mother riding on my father's shoulders. One night in a town in New Hampshire the bicycle fell . . ."

Her voice trailed off. After a moment she went on, "My uncle, Juan Guerrero, began to train me for his knife-throwing act. All I had to do, of course, was to learn to hold very still. But I wanted him to teach me to throw, too. After a while I was quite good."

Still at that rapid pace, she described how the circus had moved from one town to another all over New England during the summer months. "Then when I was sixteen, we played two weeks in a town near Providence. I met a boy there—"

She fell silent for a moment, and I knew that she must be seeing that boy from a New England summer long ago. Then she said, "The circus moved on. By late summer I knew I was pregnant.

"Uncle Juan was furious, of course. But even if I had told him the boy's name, and I wouldn't, I doubt that he could have forced the boy to marry me. He was well under age. In fact, he was four months younger than I was. I had my baby, a boy, the next February. The circus was in Georgia then, in winter quarters. Uncle Juan arranged a private adoption through a doctor. They were a very nice couple. The husband was a lawyer, from a very wealthy family. They promised me that from time to time they would send news of my little boy. In return, I had to sign a promise that I would never try to see him or even get in touch with him. You see, they had decided not to let him know he was adopted.

"When the circus went on its summer tour, Uncle Juan and I went with it. We did that for five more summers. Then, in a little

Connecticut town, Lakerton, the circus manager ran off with the receipts, leaving all of us stranded. Uncle Juan stayed long enough to get me settled in a job as a domestic, about the only work I could handle. Then he went down to New London and shipped on a freighter as an ordinary seaman. He never wrote to me, but five years later I received a letter from a shipmate of his. It said that my uncle had died of pneumonia in Bremen, Germany."

She went on talking of her years with the Covarrubias family, the people with whom her uncle had placed her. They were well-to-do people, she said, and quite haughty about their descent from Spanish grandees. "But they were very nice to me. After a while I did very little housework. Instead I spent most of my time caring for their little boy. Part of the reason, I guess, was that I spoke Spanish as well as English, and they wanted their son to grow up speaking both languages."

I said, in a strained voice, "Their son? Manuelo?"

"Yes. He was only two when I came to work for them. As you can imagine, he was about the most beautiful two-year-old boy alive. I was crazy about him. I guess he was sort of a substitute for the little boy I'd had to give up.

"But I still had news of my son," she went on. "That couple still sent me regular reports on his progress. They had named him Jerome, and on each of his birthdays they sent me a picture of him."

That rapid voice went on, recounting how she'd stayed with the Covarrubias family all through Manuelo's growing years, and after he went away to college and medical school. "He was with the Army Medical Corps in Vietnam for a while. When he came back, he opened his plastic surgery practice in a duplex apartment in Manhattan, with his living quarters on the second floor. He wanted me to keep house for him. Mr. and Mrs. Covarrubias said it was all right, so I did."

And when, several years later, he told her that he planned to open a sanatorium in central California, she was more than eager to come with him. "You see, I knew I wouldn't be far from San Jose."

"San Jose?"

"Yes. I knew that that Georgia couple had gone out to California years before for the wife's health, taking little Jerome with them, of course. Only he was no longer little. He had grown up, and married, and had a daughter."

I asked sharply. "What was their name, the people who adopted your baby son?"

"Why, it's Montgomery. Didn't I tell you?"

"No, you didn't tell me."

She went on, recounting how she had accompanied Manuelo to Serena, and how, because they both thought it would sound more dignified, she had begun to call herself Mrs. Guerrero.

Quite suddenly, her voice became dull and flat. "Only a few years after I came out here, Jerome's wife died, and he and his little girl Gabriella moved back into the house where he had grown up. And the year after that my son shot himself through the head."

For a moment the room was silent. Then she said, "I'd always kept that written agreement of mine about not getting in touch with Jerome in any way. Oh, after I came to California I used to make trips to San Jose and go past the house where Jerome and his wife and little girl lived. Later, after he and his daughter moved back to the house where he'd grown up, I'd go past that house.

"But after he killed himself, I felt I had to see my granddaughter, I *had* to. I realized

I would be breaking my agreement to keep my distance from the Montgomery family, but I had to do it.

"I went there early one afternoon, when I was sure Gabriella would still be at the day school they sent her to. Mrs. Montgomery opened the door. It sounds strange, considering that we hadn't seen each other since I was seventeen and she was twenty-seven, but we knew each other right off. She wasn't angry with me for coming there, not at all. Right there in the hall we fell into each other's arms and cried and cried.

"Gabriella came home about an hour later. In the very first moment I knew I loved her. Loved her more than my own child . . . the child I knew I must not love too much because he would be taken from me at birth. I loved her even more than Manuelo, because after all he was not my own flesh and blood.

"Mrs. Montgomery said to her, 'This is Mrs. Guerrero, an old, old friend of mine. You can call her Aunt Maria, if you like.'

"I went there often after that. Gabriella seemed to grow fond of me. She was an unusually quiet child—and no wonder, with the tragedy she'd had in her young life—but she got so she'd chatter away to me about her tennis lessons, and her classmates, and, later on, the college applications she was going to send out now that she'd reached her last year of prep school. She and I went shopping together, and to the movies. She even spent a few hours of each Christmas Day here, at that big open house Manuelo gave each year. And then there was that last Christmas party—"

She stopped abruptly. I said, through the pulse throbbing in the hollow of my throat. "You mean that party four years ago."

She nodded. "That was when Manuelo saw Gabriella. Oh, not that he hadn't seen her lots of other times before. But then she had seemed to him just a child. Now he was seeing her as a beautiful young woman. I could tell. God knows I had seen That look on his face often enough. Maybe *you* didn't realize what was happening, but I did."

No, I thought, with the metallic taste of an old bitterness in my mouth, I hadn't realized. I had been too busy seeing to it that my mother had a good time, too busy playing the piano during the intervals between Patrick Murray's wailing bagpipes and that country-western band.

"I knew what that look on his face meant," she said. "Again and again I'd watched him play stupid young girls as if they were so many fish, reeling them in very carefully. Then, when the novelty wore off, he'd drop the one he had overboard and go for another one."

She threw me a look tinged with embarrassment, as if she'd suddenly recollected that I had been the last of those stupid young girls.

"I couldn't let him do that to Gabriella. After Christmas he came down with the flu, but when he got well I went to his apartment. I told him I'd kill him if he didn't leave her alone."

So it must have been Maria Guerrera quarreling with Manuelo, her voice so hoarse with rage that I had thought it might be Swedenborg in the apartment, or some other man.

"He said that with Gabriella everything would be 'different.' He said that he truly loved her and intended to marry her. I said that in the first place I didn't want my granddaughter to marry a middle-aged tomcat, and that in the second place I didn't believe that this time it would be any different. I'd known him for forty years, all but the first two years of his life. And I told him again that I'd kill him if he didn't leave her alone.

He was furious by then, so furious that he ordered me out of his apartment."

"And so," I said, slowly and bitterly, "you decided to kill him and frame *me* for it. Didn't your conscience ever bother you about that?"

A flush dyed her sallow face. "Yes, but you see, I thought the court would let you off, or at least give you only a year, a nice young girl who'd been treated the way Manuelo treated you. Believe me, I had nothing against you. I had a lot better opinion of you than of the other girls who'd caught his eye from time to time. But all that was really important to me was Gabriella. If I were arrested for doing what had to be done, everything about me would come out. Gabriella would know that she was the granddaughter of a murderess. And that I couldn't bear. Besides, it was so . . . so logical that you might have been the one to kill him. You certainly had the motive. He'd thrown you over. And you had plenty of opportunity."

"And you clinched it," I said, in that same bitter voice, "by getting my fingerprints onto that knife handle. First you drugged some food and put it in my room. I thought it was Amy who had put that ham sandwich and milk in my room, but it was you, wasn't it?"

"Yes. I mixed barbiturate in the milk. Of course I couldn't be sure you'd drink it, but you did. About four o'clock, with a knife from that display case in my skirt pocket, I went to your room. I knocked, and when there was no answer I went in. You were fast asleep. I wrapped your fingers around the knife handle. Then, holding it by the blade, I went back to my room.

"When I heard Manuelo open his door across the hall, I went to his apartment and told him again that he must leave my granddaughter alone. He just turned his back on me, and I threw the knife. I wasn't sure I could do it after all these years, but it found its mark. Well, that's all."

She looked exhausted, yet strangely peaceful. Again I had a feeling that in a way she had welcomed the opportunity to tell her story.

"Not quite all," I said. "I want to know about last night."

"About how I drugged you? It was simple. I told poor dumb Irene that you were a very important person indeed, and that I wanted to inspect the food she took to you. She brought your tray to my room. It was no

286

trick at all to slip the drug—a very heavy dose, this time—into that tureen."

I nodded. A dose heavy enough that I had been unable to resist as she unwound the gauze from my face. "What made you first suspect—"

"That you were Sara Hargreaves? Nothing strange about that. As soon as I heard you'd escaped I became afraid you'd turn up here. Then Dr. Swedenborg arrives with a mystery patient. More than that, there was something familiar about the way you walked, and certain gestures of yours. All I had to do was make sure I was right.

"Once I'd found out you really were Sara Hargreaves, I still didn't know what to do about it. I couldn't know how much you knew about me or had guessed. If you still had no idea of the truth, it might be all right to call the police anonymously and tell them where they could pick you up. But if you *had* managed to gather some information that could point to me . . ."

She paused for a few moments and then said, "I was sitting here a little while ago, trying to decide what to do, when I heard noise from the direction of your room.

"I was having trouble with the lock on my

door. I'd gotten a key that fitted it, but it was awfully hard to turn."

She nodded! "We had several earth tremors here last fall. Quite a few locks were jarred out of line. I guess no one checked that particular lock because the room was unoccupied. Anyway, even though I've gotten a little deaf over the last few years, you were making enough noise that I heard it.

"I opened my door a crack, very quietly. I saw you walk to that long window and stand there against the light, a perfect target.

"The temptation was just too great." Tension in her voice now. "I'd done it once and gotten away with it. Why not again, especially since I'd be using a knife perfectly balanced for throwing? I'd saved it from the old act as a souvenir and kept it in a drawer over there."

She nodded toward a flat-topped desk beside the door. Then she went on. "No one here except Manuelo had ever known about my days with the circus. I suppose that's why, even if it had occurred to someone that the knife might have been thrown, not driven into his back by someone's hand, they would never have suspected an old woman like me. Why should they suspect me this time?

"And as I looked at you standing there, I realized that if I passed up this chance I might never get another one. You were determined to find out what had really happened four years ago. Your coming back here proved that. And if I let you go on trying—

"I took the knife from the desk drawer and gave it a quick polish with my skirt. I stepped back into the hall, holding the knife by the blade tip, and threw it.

"Only this time," she said, her voice suddenly flat and dull, "I wasn't lucky."

She stopped speaking. The room was so silent that I could hear the voices of men in the long garage behind the sanatorium. Then I said, "We're going to my room."

She looked at me questioningly. For answer, I just waved the gun slightly. She got up, walked ahead of me down the hall to my door. "Just go in," I said. "The door isn't locked.

She did as I asked. I followed her. I said, "Sit down at that table beside the window."

Keeping my eye on her, I closed the door. No need to lock it, not while I held the gun. Still watching her, I backed across the room and opened the drawer in the little desk. My groping left hand picked up a ballpoint pen and several sheets of letter paper. I placed them in front of her on the table.

I sat down on the chaise longue. "Now write it all down. About Gabriella Montgomery being your granddaughter. About how you killed Manuelo and framed me for it."

For a moment something like rebellion appeared in her wretched dark eyes. Then the look died. She picked up the pen and began to write. It made no sound as it traveled over the paper. After a while, when my right hand grew tired, I shifted the gun to my left. The only sounds in the room were the voices drifting up from the lawn below, and a faint rustling when Mrs. Guerrero turned over a piece of paper.

At last she extended the pages to me. She looked utterly beaten, shoulders slumped, gaze directed at the floor. Nevertheless, I glanced at her every few seconds as, with the pages held on my lap, I skimmed through what she had written.

She had condensed her story considerably but all the essentials were there. She had written of the circus act, and of the birth of an illegitimate son who eventually became Gabriella Montgomery's father. She told of her conviction that the only way to save her granddaughter from Manuelo Covarrubias was to kill him. And she described how she had framed me for his murder.

Awkwardly I folded the pages with my left hand and thrust them into my skirt pocket. "Lie down on the bed," I said. "Face down."

She looked faintly surprised, nothing more. She moved to the bed and stretched out on her stomach. Watching her in the dressing-table mirror, I laid down the gun and picked up manicure scissors. Swiftly I cut away the gauze. Free, I thought, and not just from the bandages. Those sheets of paper in my pocket freed me from the prospect of spending many more years as I had spent the last four.

I smoothed down my hair. Then, after another glance at the motionless figure on the bed, I put the gun in my other skirt pocket. I opened the door and, after a brief struggle, managed to lock it. I hurried down the stairs, back along the broad main hall of the sanatorium, past white-clad men and women who threw me startled looks but did not challenge me. Then I saw Mike, pushing a mop over the lustrous vinyl floor.

"Mike!" He looked with startled eyes at my unbandaged face. "The most wonderful thing—"

291

He leaned his mop against the wall. "In here," he said, and drew me into an empty room. A swift glance revealed that, except for the antiseptic smell and the crank at the foot of the bed, it bore little resemblance to ordinary hospital rooms. It had silken yellow draperies, and flower prints on walls of paler yellow.

I spoke briefly, rapidly, and then handed him Maria Guerrero's confession. He skimmed through it just as rapidly, and then thrust the pages into the pocket of his white shirt. "I want to talk to her right now." Excitement had turned his face quite pale.

Still unchallenged, we went up the stairs, the back stairs this time, since they were closer. Hand unsteady, I tried to unlock the door of my room, then stepped back to let Mike manage the balky lock. He swung the door back.

The bed was empty. The whole room was empty. I stood bewildered in the middle of the floor. Mike looked into the bathroom, turned around, hesitated. I followed the direction of his gaze. Stomach tightening, I saw that the side window was open. When I left the room it had been shut.

He walked over to it, tilted the now-unlatched window screen outward and looked down. As I started to follow, he turned sharply to me. "No! Don't look."

I thought of her down there, a crumpled figure, dark against the white cement of that empty fish pond.

Horrified voices came from below now. People had found her. Mike walked toward me. He put his arms around me briefly and kissed my lips. "Wait here," he said. "I'll see if she's—"

He left me. I stood motionless in the center of the room. More sounds from below now. They would be bringing her into the building, up to the sanatorium floor.

I was sure that it wasn't fear of prison that had sent her out that window. What she could not bear was the thought of what she would see in Gabriella's eyes.

Mike came back. "She's dead, Sara."

He put his arms around me. I wept on his shoulder for Maria Guerrero, who had died rather than face horrified rejection in the face of the one person she loved.

But even as I wept, my heart was rejoicing. We could go wherever we chose now, Mike and I. And we could go together.

"They've called the police," he said. "We'd better go down."

We walked toward the door.